All rights reserved. No part of this book may be reproduced in any form by any electronic or mechanical means including photocopying, recording, or information storage and retrieval without permission in writing from the author.

Shadow Game
Paperback Copyright © 2024 Lorhainne Ekelund
Editor: Talia Leduc

All rights reserved.
ISBN-13: 978-1998354023

Give feedback on the book at:
lorhainneeckhart@hotmail.com

Twitter: @LEckhart
Facebook: AuthorLorhainneEckhart

Printed in the U.S.A

SHADOW GAME

THE WATCHERS
BOOK 1

LORHAINNE ECKHART

"What's really going on in this idyllic isolated town? Raul Booth goes looking for answers but finds more than he was bargaining for."

CATLOU

"A fantastic story of corruption at the highest level and the nefarious going on at Shadow Valley will have you gripped to the end of your seats."

C. Logue

ABOUT THE WATCHERS

Six unlikely friends, with a diverse set of skills, are brought together to face off against a common enemy in the mind-bending new series *The Watchers*.

Shadow Game

Meet the Watchers: Six unlikely people from different backgrounds united by a common goal—to make the world a better place.

One night, Raul receives a call from an old childhood friend who tells him a wild story about human experimentation in a small town deep in the Appalachian Mountains, not far from where they grew up. Raul dismisses it, but a day later, his friend is found dead in a motel room two hundred miles away.

When Raul arrives in the small town his friend described, it appears postcard perfect, as do the residents. However, as he digs into its history, he discovers that the town square is fake, the police chief harbors secrets, everyone seems related in some way, and something nefarious is occurring in the surrounding woodlands.

Then, seemingly coincidentally, Raul meets five others in town who have also noticed something off. As they join forces, they soon learn that something far more sinister is unfolding. And worse, what they uncover hits closer to home for Raul than he could have imagined. Could it be bigger than any of them are equipped to handle?

CHAPTER 1

Raul Booth felt a storm brewing even though the day was hot and sunny and the blue sky held not even a wisp of clouds. His face was damp and his bare chest sweaty, the faded old blue T-shirt he had pulled off resting over the edge of the rusty wheelbarrow. He lifted the ax and brought it down hard, splitting another round of birch, then reached for another. The echo of the sharp thud in the hills was oddly comforting.

"You want to tell me what you've got stuck in your craw? Because I'm getting tired of watching you, and as much as I appreciate the wood, I can't see myself burning all that," came the voice of his older brother, Asher, who was sitting in an old wooden chair on the porch beside Raul's dog. "Suppose I could sell some, but it doesn't seem fair, taking advantage of you this way. Let me think on that a second."

Raul rested the blade of the ax on the ground and pulled the back of his other hand over his forehead, which was dripping with sweat. He stared up at Asher; his dark hair was wavy, and his beard needed a trim.

"You know what?" Asher said. "On second thought, I won't lose any sleep, making a profit off your skinny ass. What do you suppose you've cut there for me, about six cords, seven?"

Raul gripped the wooden handle of the ax and lifted it with one hand, feeling the burn in his shoulders. He then buried the ax in the chopping block with a thud, reached down for the split wood around it, and tossed it onto the pile he had chopped. "Figured it's the least I can do since you're feeding me and letting me bunk down here."

The quietness that settled as he tossed the last piece of wood had him wiping his hands and turning around. His brother was watching him with the same sadness he'd tried to hide since Raul had shown up two weeks earlier. "Stay, my ass, Raul. This is always your home. You're not a damn guest here, you know that, especially considering you're bunking down in the old shed on a cot with the dog. Again, how about you come clean on what's eating you? You've been chopping since sun-up. I made coffee hours ago and even a sandwich, expecting you'd come in when you were hungry, but I'm starting to think you enjoy discomfort. For two days, all you've done is chop as if you're a damn machine."

Raul let his gaze settle on his mutt of a dog, who was resting on the shady porch, watching him with mud-brown eyes. "I'm not complaining," he said. "It's my way of saying thanks for keeping my dog when I'm gone."

His brother was leaning back now in the old wooden chair, lifting the front legs off the porch, rocking it a bit, as he looked down at the dog. "Yeah, well, you had to pick a lazy thing. Doesn't even carry his weight, just eats and sleeps. You couldn't even give it a halfway decent name..."

"He's got a name. Dawg."

He never could tell when his brother was smiling behind that beard. Asher shook his head as he let the front of the chair down with a thunk and stood. Dawg wagged his tail from the shade of the porch, then walked to his bowl and lapped up the last of his water before picking up the bowl with his teeth and letting it fall with a thud on the old wood porch.

"Okay, boy, I hear you," Raul said. "Water break it is." He reached for his T-shirt and pulled it on. His worn jeans were covered in bits of wood and bark, hanging low on his hips as he started back to the small cabin that was his refuge. The place was hard to get to in the hills of eastern Tennessee. He stepped up onto the old porch, sheltered and shady, just as Asher started down the steps beside him. His baggy worn jeans needed a wash, and his blue T-shirt had faded to more of a pale gray.

"Go eat the sandwich I made you and get your dog some water," Asher said.

Raul opened the door to the cabin, revealing the old woodstove and the sofa his brother often fell asleep on, then turned back to his eight-year-old dog, who had the ears of a Shepherd and the coat of a brown Lab. He reached down for the metal bowl his dog had dropped and then started inside toward the small kitchen, with one counter, an old electric stove, a forty-year-old fridge that still ran, and a porcelain sink that was rusty on the sides.

The bedroom his brother had shared with his wife before she'd left was closed, and the two bedrooms off the back of the house where his five kids had slept were empty. Raul felt the heaviness that still weighed on his brother as he turned on the tap, hearing the rattle of the pipes.

The old rotary rang. He turned off the tap and set the half-full bowl on the dirty linoleum for his dog as the yellow phone rang again. He stared only a second before he reached for it, wondering who would be calling, considering the phone never rang.

"Hello? This is Raul."

There was static on the other end. "Raul, is that you? It's Wyatt. I'm in a shitload of trouble. I saw something I know I wasn't supposed to see. You're the first person I thought of calling. There's no one else. I didn't know if you'd be at your brother's or where you'd be." Wyatt Clinton, a childhood friend he hadn't seen in two years, sounded freaked out. He was rambling, and the line was cutting in and out. "God damn, they're fucking with people here. I know this is going to sound crazy, but I just walked into this place I swear was never here before. I'm not crazy, I'm not, but everything here, it's absolutely nothing like how it first looks…"

"Wyatt, Wyatt, look, slow down," Raul said. "Where are you? You're making no sense. What place?"

There was static again, and he didn't know whether it was from his end or Wyatt's. "Remember that valley not far from where we grew up, on the other side of the ridge? It was impossible to get to, and we were told to stay away when we were young. Remember the Rollins kid who disappeared, and the stories we heard about Ralph Miller going out hunting and never coming back?"

Raul had to think. There were a few places in the hills that they'd steered clear of, both inaccessible and rumored to be filled with unexplainable, dangerous shit that one didn't mess with. Superstition had been part of the community he'd grown up in. "Vaguely, sure," he said, "but what is this about? What kind of trouble are you in?

You need to be a little more specific. You need me to come and get you?"

"Look, just listen, Raul," Wyatt said. "I was checking some of my traps, and a few were completely trashed. You know I see red about that kind of shit. You never mess with a man's traps. So I followed the tracks. Just on the other side of the mountain, in the valley, there's a small town that was never there before. I know this is going to sound crazy, but I just walked in. The sign says Shadow Valley, but it's nothing I've ever seen on a map. On the surface it seems all pretty and welcoming, but there's crazy-ass shit going on there. It's like a giant experiment. They're fucking with people's heads.

"I walked into a family cafe, and everyone was staring. I asked for a coffee, and it was poured and handed to me, no charge, and I was sent on my way. I didn't have to go too far before I spotted buses pulling in with blacked-out windows. I don't think I was supposed to see any of it. I'm not kidding, I saw someone dead. In the forest were two guys with lab coats and two women sitting at a table with a gun, taking turns pulling the trigger at each other. The guys had clipboards, and after so many turns the gun went off and killed one of the women. There was blood and shit. They carried her into a small concrete building through a metal door. It just has to go underground, like nothing I've ever seen. This is completely fucked up. The other woman just sat there as if she were some damn robot.

"I cased the town, circled it, just watching from the trees. Then I went out a little farther. It scared the ever-living shit out of me, Raul. They were all smiles and hellos, the prettiest, cleanest place ever, but I swear to God, none of this can be real. There's something evil here. I know this sounds crazy, like some demented conspiracy, but it's not. I swear, Raul, there's something off. This town doesn't exist on any map of Appalachia. I know. I checked."

A chill ran down Raul's spine. "Just back up, there. Are you sure you haven't been smoking something?"

"For fuck's sake, Raul, I'm stone-cold sober. I'm telling you what I see here makes my skin crawl and scares the shit out of me. It's sick and twisted…"

Behind him, his dog was lapping up water, and outside his brother was whistling. He tried to make sense of what his childhood friend was saying. He rubbed his head, feeling his disheveled wavy brown hair, which he'd only run a comb through so many days ago.

"Well, first, getting the hell out of there would be the smartest thing to do," Raul said. "You know as well as I do that there could be a hundred different explanations for whatever it is you think you saw out there." But even as the words passed his lips, he didn't believe them. He'd learned that people did crooked, evil things for money and reasons he no longer tried to understand.

"Yeah, well, you tell me a reason that makes a lick of sense," Wyatt said. "I'm already making my way back. You know I'm not some dumbass. Just tell me, you worked for the CIA, the military, all that shit. Do they know about this kind of thing? It's not on a map. I'm telling you, this is spooky. Nothing scares me, but right now, I'm freaking out."

The phone line was cutting out, static again. Raul thought of everything the government could have its hand in. The power of the state was something he'd stopped talking about long ago. "It could be, or it could be something else entirely," he said. "Just get the fuck out of there."

"What do you think I'm doing? I'm moving my ass as I'm talking to you. But what about this place, these people, what I saw? I'm not sure about the bus, but I saw kids and families getting off. Then this black-robed guy showed up like it's fucking Halloween..."

Raul's mind raced, and he made himself pull in one breath and another. Wyatt was as steady as they came, but his voice revealed the gravity of the situation and the implications of what he'd shared. Raul knew he couldn't simply dismiss his friend's claims. After a moment of silence and more static, he took a deep breath and responded, his voice filled with concern.

"Wyatt, listen to me carefully. If it's what you're saying, then you don't want to be found there."

"It's exactly as I'm saying." Wyatt cut him off, and the edge in his voice came through clearly. "I took photos, lots."

Raul took a second to realize what his friend had said. If Wyatt was right, this wasn't the kind of thing anyone lived to talk about, let alone show photos of. "Fine, you get your ass back here. Keep your head down, and shut your phone down as soon as we finish talking. You call no one else and talk to no one. You hear me? If what you're saying is true, then we're dealing with something dangerous and potentially life-threatening."

Asher, still whistling, was coming closer.

"I'm going to have a word with Asher, see what he knows about the area you're talking about. How long do you think it will take you to get here?"

There was static again, and he couldn't make out what Wyatt was saying.

"Wyatt, you're cutting out. "Listen, just come right

here. Again, talk to no one about this. You hear me, Wyatt?"

The line went dead.

"What the hell is that about?"

Raul hadn't heard his brother come in. He hung up the old phone. "I have no idea. Wyatt Clinton is on his way here. Remember the valley on the other side of the hills, west of here, where we were told never to go? Well, he went, following some tracks after a few of his traps were wrecked. He says he stumbled on a town. He's going on about weird, crazy stuff. He sounded scared in a way I've not heard him sound before."

Asher made a face as he walked over to the counter and gestured to the plate where sat a white-bread bologna sandwich, mustard seeping out of the sides. "Eat your sandwich," was all he said before starting to the closed door of his bedroom.

Raul reached for the sandwich and took a bite, tasting the stale bread as he chewed.

Asher stopped with his hand on the doorknob. "You know, Raul, there's a reason we don't go places we're told to stay out of," he said. He glanced Raul's way with an odd expression. "Raul, when you leave here and go wherever you go, I get down on my knees and pray you'll come back safe and unscathed. When you show up, I can let go of the weight that hangs around me the entire time you're gone, doing God knows what. You think I don't know the things you've seen, the things you've done? You can't hide it from me. I see your face, the scars you think you hide. You carry the weight of the world, and I can guess at what it is you've seen from the screams I hear when you've had a bad dream. I remind myself there are some things I don't want to know about, even though I probably already do. You can't fix the world, Raul. There are bad people doing evil, fucked-up shit out there."

He hadn't realized his brother heard him when he woke from the living nightmares that followed him into his dreams. His dog did, he knew, because it was Dawg who woke him each time, licking his face. He said nothing.

Asher opened the bedroom door and looked back at him again. "Maybe one day you'll come clean and tell me what has you screaming in the middle of the night. I don't want you getting killed, Raul. Whatever Wyatt stumbled upon, how about you turn it over to someone else and let that person handle it?"

Then Asher stepped into his bedroom and closed the door, and for the first time ever, Raul realized that the world of hurt he carried was likely nothing compared to his brother's pain.

The storm Raul had felt brewing earlier brought a flash of lightning that lit up the room. Heavy clouds of darkness passed across the window, and a boom of thunder that echoed in the hills had Dawg hiding in a corner. Raul stared at the phone, then at his brother's closed door, unable to shake a feeling of darkness that he couldn't make any sense of.

CHAPTER 2

The thunderous roar of the storm echoed through the valley as a torrent of rain pummeled the ground. Flashes of lightning illuminated the treeline, while gusts of wind ripped through the treetops and shook the ground beneath Raul's feet. The power of a storm was something he both respected and feared. He pulled his arms over his chest, feeling the chill the sudden storm had brought, as he leaned against the post of the covered porch, gazing out onto a landscape transformed into an eerie sea of mud and streams. The woodstove crackled in the background as darkness consumed the sky, and soon enough, even the once empty rain barrels were overflowing from the sheer force of the downpour.

"Still no sign of Wyatt? You know, with this storm, he probably took shelter," Asher said, the old porch creaking under his feet. The scent of burning wood drifted through the open door of the cabin.

Raul gazed at the dark mass of trees ahead, his unease growing as he caught a whiff of the damp earth and moldy foliage. "Not Wyatt. He's dealt with worse, hiked through worse. He knows these hills better than anyone. I'm more worried about what he saw. You have an idea about this place he hiked into, Shadow Valley?" Raul glanced back at Asher, whose expression seemed to carry all the world's worries, then at his dog, lying by the fire in the doorway. "One thing I know about Wyatt: if he says he'll be here, no force in this world is gonna stop him."

Asher shook his head slowly, then shrugged. "Foolish…" He paused and took a deep breath. "Look, all I can tell you about that place is that I heard the same as you, some strange stories a while back. I don't want to know. I have enough problems on my plate. My advice to you is don't go poking around there. When Wyatt gets back, remind him of all those warnings we heard. When someone tells you not to go near a house on a hill, or to one side of a valley, listen. There are some things you have no business messing with."

Raul thought his brother had changed so much, being away for so long. At one time, overly cautious was not how he would have described Asher.

"Maybe we should talk about Lydia and the children, why she left and where she is now," Raul said. "You haven't said a word to me about that. Have you even tried to see your kids? Do you know where they are?"

Asher was so damn stubborn in his anger, like no one Raul had ever come across. "You first," he said. "Tell me about the nightmares that have you screaming like a scared little kid." His brother edged closer, and Raul didn't appreciate being put on the spot. "Yeah, just as I thought. Best to leave some wounds alone. You do you and I'll do me."

Raul furrowed his brow and shook his head, knowing Asher's attempts to deflect the conversation could turn nasty. That was just what he did when someone picked at a wound that was still festering. It was something that seemed to run in the family. "You know, Asher, we have to talk about Lydia and the kids at some point. I can see it's eating you alive."

Asher remained silent for a moment, not looking in Raul's direction. He finally turned slowly and heaved a heavy sigh. "I don't know what happened. Sure, we fought. What couple doesn't? She talked nonsense, needing space, needing more, wanting more…" He pulled his arms over his broad chest. "One day she was just gone without a trace. Took the kids with her. No note, no explanation. I tried calling her parents, but they said they hadn't heard from her, either. It's like she vanished into thin air. I've looked everywhere, asked everyone I could think of. But nothing. I came back from hunting, gone for a day, and found empty drawers and an empty house." His words hung in the air.

"What happened? Why'd she leave? They're your kids, too, Asher, and you and Lydia, you two have known each other since forever. This makes no sense. I thought she was close with her parents. Wouldn't they know where she is?"

Asher's eyes had always been so warm and inviting, but now they held a harshness that made Raul uneasy. As he exhaled, he seemed to force tension out of his body. "Sometimes life is unfair, Raul. And her parents, well, let's just say that closeness fell away years ago, the moment she said 'I do.' They wanted better for her, and that wasn't me. Maybe they do know where she is, but they're not telling me. As far as they're concerned, she's better off without me," he said gruffly. "People can disappoint us, and we have to accept it. Not much we can do to change it. Guess I never really knew Lydia.

"I hope Wyatt finds somewhere safe to stay tonight. You should probably stay with the dog in one of the kids' rooms. There are no leaks in this house, but that shed you like so much has too many holes in the roof. You won't get any sleep if you stay out there, only get drenched." Asher gave Raul's shoulder a brotherly pat before he trudged back into the cabin.

The wind whistled through the trees, making Raul shiver as he rubbed his bare arms, letting his brother's words sink in. He hoped Lydia's folks weren't the reason she'd left with the kids. But, again, some of the things people did no longer surprised him.

Raul rested his hand on the heavy post of the porch, staring at the darkened treeline. A wave of dread washed over him as he considered Wyatt's words and the strange town he had stumbled upon. He knew the average person had no idea of the crazy shit that went on, sometimes in their own backyard. He had learned long ago that he could never talk about it. He really hoped Wyatt was wrong.

Images of the things he'd seen flooded his mind, and he shut his eyes, pushing the horrors away.

"He's gone crazy, that's all. He spends too much time in these hills alone," he muttered. He really hoped that was all it was, knowing Wyatt would take off in the middle of nowhere for weeks on end. He'd been doing it forever. Raul knew well what happened to soldiers in prolonged isolation. Just maybe, the grueling life they had lived had finally taken its toll. He hoped more than anything that what Wyatt had stumbled upon was nothing more than a few eccentric locals in a backwater town.

"Please, I need a break. No more weird shit, please," he whispered uneasily into the wind. Then he fisted his hand, slapped the post, and took in the old shed that was his refuge. Maybe his brother was right. He'd sleep in the house tonight, and for one night, maybe he'd tell himself it would be okay to be comfortable.

CHAPTER 3

T he first thing Raul noticed when he opened his eyes was the bright sun streaming through the window over the comfort of the double bed. His dog was at his feet, watching him, and he felt more rested than he had in a long time. Okay, maybe Asher had been right, but he waited another second for the guilt to hit. Penance was all he believed he was entitled to.

He pulled his hand over his face and sat up, tossing back the covers, then set his bare feet on the floor. The clatter of the stove and the smell of a strong brew of coffee told him his brother was already up. He pulled his jeans from the old blue dresser and stepped into them over his striped boxers, then strode barefoot to the bedroom door and pulled it open, smelling the sizzle of bacon.

Just then, the old rotary phone started ringing. Asher reached for it. "Morning," he said into it, his back to Raul. Then he turned his head as if he'd heard him. "Yeah, yeah, he's right here." Asher held out the phone to him with an odd look. "Knoxville police are looking for you."

Raul knew he frowned as he reached for the phone. "This is Raul Booth. Who am I speaking to?"

"Mr. Booth, this is Detective Pearle, with the Knoxville Police Department. I'm looking into a man found dead in a motel room by housekeeping. We found your name and number on him."

Raul could feel his brother staring at him. The sick feeling that weighed heavy inside him returned. "My name? I'm sorry, who did you say you found?"

"The ID says Wyatt Clinton."

He tried to picture the lady cop on the other end as he turned away from his brother and pulled his hand roughly across his forehead. No, no, this couldn't be true. Wyatt was supposed to be on his way there.

"I'm sorry, there must be a mistake. Wyatt was on his way here last night, but the storm would have held him up. It can't be Wyatt. Knoxville is two hundred miles away from us. There's no way. Someone must have stolen his ID or something. Can you send me a photo of the body you found? Look, here is my cell number." He rattled off his number before letting the phone fall away from his mouth and turning to Asher. "Can you grab my cell phone? It's tucked in the side of my bag."

"What's going on, Raul?" Asher said.

"A body found with Wyatt's ID."

Asher hesitated only a second before hurrying past him and soon returned with the phone, which Raul immediately powered on. The text message came through. He knew his brother was right there as he stared at the image of his childhood friend, looking like he was asleep. His heart sank in his chest. He knew the difference. He was staring at a dead man.

"Yeah, fuck, that's him," he said. "This makes no sense.

I spoke with him yesterday afternoon. He was on his way here..." He stopped talking. The last thing he wanted to share with a cop he didn't know was how freaked out his friend had been over what he'd discovered. "What happened to him? You said housekeeping found him?"

Asher set a hand on his shoulder. He had noticed what Raul hadn't said, that Wyatt was dead.

"I'm sorry, but I can't tell you more than that since it's an ongoing investigation," Detective Pearle said. "Do you have any idea why Wyatt would be in Knoxville or who he was seeing there? Does he have family? Was he meeting with anyone?"

Raul stared at the picture of his deceased friend on his cell phone. He sensed Asher looking over at him from where he had stepped away to lift the skillet of bacon from the stove. "No idea why he'd be in Knoxville. I know his parents retired and moved to Irvine, Kentucky. Beth and Stanley Clinton. I'm not sure what else I can tell you other than that Wyatt and I were friends."

"If you think of anything else useful, such as enemies or reasons why he'd be here, please call me back at this number," was all the detective said, then rattled off the number and hung up.

Raul nodded silently, typing the number into his cell phone contact list, before placing the receiver in its cradle. For a moment, it was hard for him to breathe. Sorrow overcame him, and the reality of Wyatt's death hit him like a landslide.

"Raul, what's going on?" Asher finally asked.

Raul powered off his cell phone, wiping away the image he had been looking at. "Wyatt was found dead in a motel room in Knoxville. That's roughly two hundred miles away. This doesn't make a lick of sense. He was on his way here."

There had to be more to the story. The circumstances surrounding Wyatt's death were too bizarre, too sudden.

He didn't miss the confusion staring back at him. Asher frowned, letting out a sigh of frustration. "What was Wyatt doing all the way in Knoxville? He hated cities more than anyone else I know. He would never go somewhere like that on his own."

Raul turned to the open door of the cabin, surprised to see his dog walking back in. The sun shone through the doorway, promising another warm day. "Wyatt is a seasoned hunter and trapper. He chose a life out here, living in a cabin he built with his own two hands. Yet, somehow, he wound up in a motel in Knoxville right after he called me, freaking out about this mysterious town in the part of the valley we were warned to stay out of as kids. Even you, last night, were warning me to sit Wyatt down and give him a talking-to as if he were some wet-behind-the-ears kid who should know better. Something doesn't smell right here, and everything points to that town. What was it...?" He pressed his thumb and forefinger to the bridge of his nose and then let his hand fall away, taking in his big brother, who appeared to carry the weight of the world. "If I've learned one thing, it's that there's no such thing as coincidence, none. So whatever happened to Wyatt has everything to do with that mysterious town he walked into. Shadow Valley." He pressed his lips together, thinking, and then turned back to the sofa, the table, the bookcase against the wall. "You have a map? I need to get a better idea of where this is."

Asher strode across the room and pulled out a drawer in an old desk by the wood stove, then walked back over to the kitchen table and pushed aside some mail and papers. As Raul unfolded the outline of the Appalachian Mountains and the adjacent states, Asher handed him a cup of steaming coffee.

"Thank you," Raul said.

His brother pulled in a breath and gestured down at the map. He pressed his index finger to an obscure spot in the hilly terrain that they typically stayed away from. "Look around here. If that town exists, it would be there. I'm not convinced, but then again, I learned to stay out of unhealthy places, if you know what I mean. I'll put some eggs on for you," Asher said, then walked back over to the old stove and reached for the cast iron fry pan.

Raul let his brother's meaning sink in. "You heard something, then? Come on, Asher. This is me. You're the one who lives here. I've got my focus everywhere else."

Asher didn't turn around, but he sensed him tensing up. "You mean you're distracted, seeing things that steal your peace. Sounds kind of like what Wyatt found. I've heard enough to know that I don't want to know more. Danger, trouble, watch your back, and stay the fuck away." Asher reached for the eggs, and Raul realized that was all he was going to get from him.

"Tell me more about this town you found, Wyatt," Raul mumbled while examining the map laid out on the kitchen table. He wanted to know what had frightened his friend so much. Terror and fear could go right through a man, Raul knew. He reached for a pencil among the stack of papers and unopened mail, then circled the area Asher had indicated. The scent of cooked eggs combined with freshly brewed coffee wafted through the air. Raul knew that when a place wasn't supposed to exist to the average person, some powerful people were likely behind it. He took a long sip of coffee, trying to calm his nerves, trying to get his head together.

"Hey, Raul," Asher said, breaking him from his thoughts, "don't blame yourself for Wyatt. That's not on you. Wyatt shouldn't have gone in there. None of this is on you."

He couldn't look at his brother as he stared at the map, feeling the unease that was always with him. "I need to go to Shadow Valley."

"No way," Asher replied sharply, as if he could control what Raul would do. "You think you're some kind of superhero or something? You need to leave this one alone. If going to that town got Wyatt killed, I don't want the same thing happening to you. I have enough trouble as it is." He scooped up eggs and bacon and dumped them on a plate, then reached for a fork and held the lot out to him. "Eat your breakfast. If you want to talk about Lydia, we can do that. But I heard what you were saying about the wacky experiments Wyatt was talking about—people killing each other…"

"So you're lecturing me now? I can't just sit and do nothing, Asher. Wyatt's dead, and I need to find out what happened." Raul felt his brother's angst and worry. "Look, I may not be good at a lot, or educated with some fancy degree, but I am good at handling things. I'm not walking in blind. I'll have both eyes wide open. This is what I do. I'm not turning my back on Wyatt. He was killed over something he saw, something he wasn't supposed to see. I'm more convinced than ever, and I'm damn sure going to find out what it was."

"I understand that, Raul, but you can't just go charging into that town. It's dangerous, and it's just as likely I'll get a call next, saying you've been found dead in some roadside motel," Asher snapped, his tone serious, his face red now from anger. Emotion had spiked the tension in the small room.

Raul pulled in a breath, seeing how unsteady his brother was. He had to remind himself to stay calm. "Hey, Asher, I'll be careful. I'm just going to poke around a bit, see what I can see. I'm a quick study when it comes to assessing situations, and I've been in dodgy conditions more times than I can recall. Believe me that I'll use my head here."

"So that's it, you're going?"

Raul put the plate his brother had handed him down on the edge of the table. "As soon as I'm ready. You'll keep Dawg for me?"

He knew Asher was on edge from the sigh of frustration he let out before looking away. "You know I'll always look after that damn dog for you. But you hear me, Raul: You get a sniff of anything off, you hightail it the hell out of there, and you call me."

Raul was quiet for a moment, the weight of Asher's words pressing down on him.

"You want to talk about Lydia, you come back," Asher said.

With a slow nod, Raul finally said, "I'll hold you to it. When I get back, we'll sit down and really talk."

Just then, Dawg came bounding into the room, tail wagging, as if he'd realized Raul was leaving again. Raul bent down and scratched the big mutt behind his ears before standing up.

Asher reached for his own plate on the counter, eggs and bacon cold now, a fork still clenched in one hand. "Same goes, brother. You make sure you come back, and I want to know what caused those nightmares you won't talk about," Asher said. Then, without another word, he headed for the open cabin door. Before stepping outside, he called out, "Come on, Dawg."

Then his brother was gone along with his dog. Raul let his gaze linger on the open door. All that was left was his plate of eggs and bacon and a map, and all he knew was that he couldn't let this go. That wasn't how he was made. Something had happened to his friend, and he needed to figure out what. Then he would figure out justice. Though nothing else had been said, Raul understood what Asher had meant. He was worried about him.

CHAPTER 4

Raul despised long goodbyes. Enough was enough. He watched through the rear-view mirror as his brother and his faithful dog walked away. As he drove, they seemed to be moving forward, knowing he was gone. The tree-lined dirt road concealed the small house, his sanctuary, from his view. Out of sight, out of mind, or so the saying went. However, his friend's voice kept echoing in his head.

If only he could turn back time, go back a day, and tell his friend to come to him. He tried to envision the storm and what could possibly have happened to Wyatt between his hanging up the phone and his lifeless body being found in a motel room two hundred miles away. The questions of why and how haunted him. He knew he needed to speak to that detective again, but first he needed to uncover what his friend had seen, what had terrified him so profoundly.

Raul drove past the only turn he ever took, leading him back to the highway. He continued down a winding, narrow country road lined with trees, a mix of gravel and dirt with occasional ruts. It felt unfamiliar, especially as he rounded a bend and stumbled upon a country gas station and store seemingly out of nowhere. The small clapboard store looked even older than the single decades-old pump. He pulled up in his nearly full pickup, turned off the engine, and stepped out with a rusty squeal of the door.

He always carried two jerry cans of gas. One was empty and the other full, so Raul reached for the empty one. As he walked around his pickup, he took in the faded white store with a framed single-pane window. He heard nothing but a low electrical hum and the sound of the breeze rustling the trees. His instincts, which had saved him time and again, urged him to be cautious. He glanced around, noting the old wooden screen door. He pulled it open and stepped inside.

The creak of the old wood floor greeted him as he encountered a rack of pamphlets for excursions and places to visit, dollar store trinkets, and a wall with crates of fresh vegetables and fruits. Shelves held camping supplies. The floor squeaked behind him, and he turned to see a woman of average height, in her early fifties, with brown shoulder-length hair and glasses. She wore a worn blue sweater.

"Can I help you?" Her voice had a familiar twang, and her smile, while polite, didn't seem entirely warm.

Raul held up the jerry can. "I just need to fill my gas can. I had no idea this place was here. It's cute."

She kept her gaze steady, and the formal smile faded. She said nothing but leaned against the counter, crossing her arms. A chill seemed to come from nowhere. "You can pay afterward. Go ahead, fill it up." She tilted her head toward the pump, and the smile returned, but her gaze remained fixed on him.

Raul let his gaze linger for a moment. There was no

cash register, no computer. Everything about this place felt old-school. "I can do that. Do you get many visitors here? I can't imagine you'd see many." He glanced behind him, looking for a security mirror or cameras, but found nothing.

"Now and then. What brings you out this way?" She was smiling again, but her crooked bottom teeth and the unnerving quiet made Raul uneasy.

"My family has a home in the hills not far from here, but I've never ventured out this way. Maybe you can help me with something. I received a call from a friend who stumbled upon a place in the valley over there. We were always told not to go over there, growing up. You know all that superstitious stuff. But something strange happened. My friend found a town down in that valley, but it doesn't exist on any map. A new development, maybe, in this area? Do you happen to know what he's talking about, by any chance?"

She didn't blink, only took a breath before shaking her head. "I can't help you there. Sounds like your friend might have gotten lost or turned around. There are a few new places being built, some big homes, but that's it. Not much out this way. Feel free to come back after you've filled up your gas can, and we'll settle up."

He filled his gas can and returned to the counter, where the woman was holding an iPad. He reached for his wallet and handed her a twenty.

"One more question: how far does this road go? I can't seem to get a signal, and my online map isn't working."

She opened a cashbox and gave him back his change, then waved her hand. "We're pretty much in the middle of nowhere. Cell service comes and goes. That's probably why a few folks out this way visit here, to get away from it all. The road winds for a few miles to some farms and acreages, a favorite fishing spot for the locals, and it pretty much ends at private property. That's about it. Not many people come this way unless they know someone. My advice would be to turn around and head back to the highway. There's not much else to see, and it's a waste of gas."

Raul found her response odd and realized he might not glean anything more from her. As he left, he pulled out his cellphone and snapped a photo of the small one-stop gas station and store. He couldn't shake the uneasy feeling as he slid behind the wheel of his truck, started it, and pulled back onto the winding road. He hadn't seen another vehicle in a while, and he scanned the forest on either side as he drove, taking in the various shades of green that painted the mountainside.

After a few minutes, Raul encountered a dead end, with a metal forestry gate blocking the way ahead. He slowed down and stopped a few yards from it. He stared for a moment, not wanting to turn back. The gate wasn't locked, and a sign was nailed to a tree nearby, partially hidden by a heavy branch covered in foliage.

PRIVATE PROPERTY. NO TRESPASSING.

"WELL, WELL." HE DIDN'T SEE ANY CAMERAS, SO HE PUSHED the gate open before returning to his idling pickup and driving through it. He continued down the road, which was surprisingly well maintained despite its apparent lack of use. The trees formed a dense canopy above him, creating a surreal atmosphere. As he drove, the gravel road narrowed, but as he rounded a bend, it transitioned into a paved road with a freshly painted yellow line. A yellow sign warned of caution ahead. Raul drove on, eventually passing another sign that read, "Welcome to Shadow Valley."

"What the heck?" His chest tightened and his heart raced as he gripped the steering wheel. He couldn't believe his eyes. He had stumbled upon a town that seemed as picture-perfect as Wyatt had described it, as if it had been plucked from a postcard. It was small, quaint, clean.

Raul parked his truck in front of a well-maintained grassy park alongside the road. Not a single car was in sight. Nearby, a man sat outside a coffee shop, and a woman washed the windows of a small storefront. The feeling that he was not supposed to be there was hard to shake.

He stepped out of his truck, pulled on his mud brown windbreaker, and felt a chill in the air that reminded him of mountain towns where it was winter for ten months of the year. As he walked toward the small cafe, its open sign flashing, the man sitting outside gave him an odd look.

"Are you lost or something?" the man asked. The woman, with brown hair pulled back and mismatched brows, had also turned to look at him inquisitively.

Raul found himself saying, "No, I'm not lost. I believe I might be exactly where I'm supposed to be."

CHAPTER 5

"And where do you think you should be?" the man said, his eyes locking on to Raul's. He sported a gray zip-up light jacket. A cup of coffee, its empty creamer and sugar packet beside it, sat before him. He had already taken a few sips.

"Well, I got a call from a buddy who stumbled upon this place. You know what's funny? Shadow Valley doesn't show up on any maps, but, man, it's pretty. Have you been here long?" Raul casually slid his hands into his pockets, feeling his cell phone, keeping an ear out for voices inside the cafe. A woman strolled out with a child in tow, strutting in heels and a green dress, with bright red lipstick and a wide smile.

"Who's your friend?" the man asked.

Raul's attention returned to him. He wasn't exactly grinning. There was something about the way he observed Raul that suggested he wasn't missing much. In the distance, a white vehicle with police lights and a sheriff's star sped past. His heart quickened. He sensed that his welcome party had arrived.

"Can I get you another coffee, Ralph?" A lady's cheerful voice filled the air. She emerged from the cafe, appearing to be in her early thirties, her hair neatly done, fresh bangs framing her face.

"Had my fill for today, Deb."

Turning to Raul, she smiled broadly, revealing perfectly straight teeth. "Can I get you something?"

"I'd love a regular coffee, a little cream, a little sugar, if that's not too much trouble," Raul replied.

She nodded and moved past him just as he heard a car door. A large, rather imposing man with a badge on his brown down vest, dark hair, a mustache, and dark glasses emerged and headed straight for Raul, and the lady from the cafe had mysteriously vanished. Raul was well acquainted with cops, and this one was clearly all about authority.

"Wyatt, that was my friend's name," Raul said.

The cop halted in front of him, revealing a name tag that read Chief Walker. His expression was stern. "You're the one inquiring about Shadow Valley?" he asked, his voice deep.

Raul had a hunch the coffee lady inside had made the call. He didn't look away even as a sense of unease settled in. "Yeah, it's a lovely, pristine town you've got here."

The chief glanced at Raul's pickup, a rusty old heap that seemed out of place in that setting. "Do you mind telling me your purpose here?" he said, his eyes scanning Raul up and down. Raul knew what he was doing, making him feel unwelcome—and it was working.

"Not sure it's any of your business, Chief Walker. Last I checked, this is still a free country." Raul wasn't sure what to make of the odd smile and rough laugh, but poking the bear would probably lead to his getting escorted out of town or worse.

"You sound like trouble, Mister..." The chief let the word linger, and Raul realized he needed to tone it down.

"Sorry, Raul Booth. I have family not far from here, on the other side of the hills. The thing is, I never even realized this town was here. It's not on any map. Pretty, clean, quiet..."

"Well, Mr. Booth, this is a peaceful place. So what's your business here?" The chief was prying, but Raul couldn't shake the feeling that some things were being kept hidden. At the same time, he had an instinct to be cautious, a gut feeling that some people weren't to be messed with.

"No real business, just passing through. Like I said, a friend told me about this place. He stumbled upon it, so I thought I'd check it out," Raul added, noticing the older man had folded his newspaper and glanced at the chief. He wasn't sure what passed between them.

"Here's your coffee," said the lady, who had reappeared. "No charge, on the house." She handed him a takeaway cup with a lid, indicating that she preferred he didn't stay.

He took the cup and gestured with it. "That's very kind of you. Thank you."

The young woman looked at the older man, who jutted his chin, and she promptly left. It begged the question, who was in charge there?

"This Wyatt have a last name?" the chief asked, and now Raul couldn't shake the feeling he was being played with, like a game of cat and mouse, and he was the mouse.

"Again, he just stumbled upon this place. He called me because I'm a former cop, did my time in the military, and spent some time out this way, so I thought I'd check it out. Seems welcoming and pretty."

The chief muttered under his breath and made a face. "Well, I'm afraid your timing is bad. This is a closed town, a small community, and we don't take kindly to strangers here. Now, Deb provided you with your coffee. I see your pickup parked over there. You should get in and turn around, head back where you came from."

"A closed town!" Raul was tempted to laugh, but he thought better of it when he realized the chief was serious. He could hear birds singing in the park and let his gaze linger on a big oak tree, full of leaves, the kind he'd climbed as a kid. "Well, if you don't mind, I think I'll stick around for a few days, get a feel for this place. Can either of you recommend a motel?"

The chief cleared his throat and caught Raul's gaze. "No motels here, Mr. Booth, and no strangers are allowed. I don't want to be impolite, but it's best if you turn back the way you came."

The older man, who was still folding up his newspaper, spoke up this time. "The chief is right. If you decide to stay, you have to abide by our town rules. We don't take kindly to newcomers, and there are certain regulations that must be followed. First, no one is allowed in the town square past nine p.m. unless they're attending a local event or function. Second, all newcomers must register with the town hall before setting up residence within the city limits. Third, weapons of any kind are not permitted within town borders unless authorized by a member of law enforcement. Finally, pickup trucks are not allowed within city limits after dark, so keep your vehicle parked outside of town until morning."

Raul looked between them as he listened and took a sip

of the coffee, which had turned bitter as it cooled. He made a face before setting the paper cup down on the round table where the older man was sitting. "Thanks for your time," was all he said, recognizing that the list of rules had been a warning more than anything else.

He headed back to his truck, crossing the road, and noticed a new white car at the end of the street, a van behind it, and a few people walking about in the town square. He had heard stories about small towns like this but had never expected to find one so isolated, off the grid, and strictly governed. He knew he should just turn around and leave while he still could, but something told him this place was worth exploring further—as long as he played by their rules. Furthermore, he was convinced that those two men knew something about what had happened to Wyatt.

CHAPTER 6

Raul's truck crept through the eerily silent town square, its engine a low rumble against the unusual picture-perfect atmosphere that enveloped the place. The square itself was an embodiment of perfection—a meticulously groomed lawn, vibrant flowerbeds, an elegant fountain as its centerpiece, and pristine white benches that seemed untouched by human hands. The surrounding buildings were equally immaculate, their bricks freshly painted, their windows shining like glass mirrors.

Yet a pervasive sense of unease hung in the air. Raul couldn't quite pinpoint the source, but the hair on the back of his neck prickled, and he had to fight the urge to roll his shoulders as he drove. It was as if the entire town held its breath, anticipating something, the kind of something he couldn't put his finger on.

"Too perfect," Raul muttered, driving slowly enough that he could see every bit of the square. "Something's off about this place. Wyatt, if you can hear me, I could use your help now, a sign or something. Who did this to you? What did you find? Where should I begin?"

As he drove out of the town, he couldn't help but notice that the old man from the cafe and the police chief had vanished, along with the patrol car.

"Where did they go?" Raul wondered aloud, gripping the steering wheel tightly. "What a pretty little place, but it's too damn perfect. What are they hiding here?"

His heart raced as he steered his truck off the main road, venturing onto a trail that led into the dense forest surrounding the town. He knew he needed a better vantage point to observe this seemingly idyllic community without drawing attention. Simultaneously, he recognized the potential threat posed by the police chief.

As the truck navigated through the thick foliage, the trees scratched its sides. Raul glanced back and realized he had veered far enough off the road to stay concealed from any passersby. He parked, switched off the engine, and quietly stepped out, listening intently for any unusual sounds, cars, or footsteps. Fortunately, the only sounds were the rustling leaves and the gentle creaking of branches.

Raul reached for his pistol and binoculars from the glovebox, holstered the gun to his jeans, and covered it with his coat. He then pocketed his keys, closed the truck door as noiselessly as possible, and ventured onto a narrow trail, his steps measured and cautious.

The foliage grew denser, and the surroundings fell into an eerie hush. Raul knew how to focus, to listen to what the average person wouldn't. At the same time, he couldn't shake the feeling of walking into a trap. When a sudden chill sent the hair on the back of his neck standing on end, he instinctively crouched low, scanning the area for signs of danger.

"Who are you?" a deep voice demanded from behind him.

Everything went into slow motion as Raul whirled around, gun in hand, standing and taking aim. He stared into the face of a stranger, taller and larger than him, his dark eyes locked on to him. The stranger had a weathered face and long, tied-back black hair. Raul hadn't even heard him approach. The man held his hands up slowly in surrender, gesturing with his chin to the gun Raul had aimed at him.

"I'll ask the same of you," Raul replied.

The man didn't move.

"Sorry, old habits," Raul said at last, withdrawing the gun, flicking off the safety, and holstering it, maintaining eye contact all the while.

"Saw you drive into town, then saw you drive out. Are you from here?" The stranger had a deep voice.

Raul shook his head. "No. I didn't even know this place existed until today. Name's Raul. And you?"

The stranger took a deep breath, lowering his hands to his sides. "Chogan Potts." He nodded at the forest around them. "So why are you sneaking around? You say you're not from here, so who are you, and what do you want? Are you a cop? You look like a cop, sound like a cop. Sneak around like a cop. You searching for something?"

Raul took his time, letting his hand linger by his gun. Who was this man, demanding answers? Again, the trap tightened around him. "I used to be a cop, among other things," he said. "I'll go out on a limb here. I heard about this place from a friend of mine who called before the storm last night. You wouldn't happen to have been around then, would you?"

Chogan's eyes narrowed, and he crossed his arms, pulling in a heavy breath. "I wasn't out during the storm. Is your friend from this town? Is that why you're here? Why don't you tell me what you're really doing here?"

Raul hesitated but didn't waver in his gaze, wondering whether checkpoints had been set up with watchers around the town. How many more were out there? "No, my friend isn't from this town. He stumbled upon it, saw something that terrified him. Now he's dead, found in a motel room in another town when he was supposed to be on his way to see me. So how about you tell me who you are and why you're here? You're out in the forest, keeping watch. This is a two-way street. I'm not from here. Are you? Why are you poking around? I'm the one doing all the talking, and it's making me pretty uneasy."

The way Chogan's dark eyes lingered on him, Raul realized the man was as closed off as he was. "No, I'm not from around here," he said after a moment. "But I've seen some strange things in my life that made no sense, and this place is one of them. You said your friend is dead, but he was here yesterday, and now here you are, sneaking around in the bush after driving into that town. So that says you're either full of shit and part of it or you suspect some foul play from this place."

Raul couldn't shake the complexity of this situation. Chogan was holding his cards close to his chest. Did he know this place or its people? Evidently more than he did, he suspected.

"Wyatt was a hunter, checking traps," Raul said. "He mentioned that someone was tampering with them, and he followed a trail that led him here. When he called me, he was in a state of panic, saying he saw something, strange things. I think he saw something he wasn't meant to see, and it terrified him. That's all that makes sense to me, because now he's dead. Were you here yesterday before the storm? Did you see a tall, lanky guy with reddish-brown hair and a beard? He's looked like that as long as I've known him."

Chogan didn't answer right away, and Raul wasn't sure what to make of how he was watching him. "I might have seen him, maybe." The last word he really emphasized as he took a step back and glanced to the side, his hands pulled tight across his chest. Then he gestured into the woods. "Let me show you something."

Without further explanation, he turned and began to walk, motioning for Raul to follow. For a second, Raul stood there. He glanced behind him, feeling the strangeness of the situation and the oddness of the man. He touched his holstered gun and then followed the trail. Chogan walked quietly, occasionally glancing back to him but saying nothing. Unnerving as all hell. This was a bad idea. The sun dipped lower in the sky, casting an amber glow on the leaves, and the silence in the forest became almost deafening, punctuated only by the distant caw of a crow and the faint whisper of the wind through the trees.

Chogan stopped in front of him and said in a low voice, "Listen." His eyes locked on to Raul's as he held a hand up as if waiting for something, or maybe someone.

Raul listened as the disconcerting silence closed in. "What are we listening for?"

Chogan's lips curled into an odd smile. "It's not always about what you hear; it's about what you don't hear. Look without your eyes. Listen. This is not a happy place. A lot of misery here. Now come on."

Raul wondered whether he'd made a face. He hesitated, really listening to the sounds of the forest, but heard nothing unusual. What was he supposed to be hearing, people or something else? He picked up his pace, following behind Chogan. The man moved a lot like Wyatt, comfortable in the woods. When the trail led them to a small clearing, Raul's breath caught in his throat. Before him lay several mounds of disturbed earth, scattered randomly. It took a moment for him to register what he was looking at.

"What the hell is this?" he murmured, recognizing them as unmarked graves hidden in the middle of nowhere. "Who…what are these?" He couldn't tear his eyes from the makeshift burial site. He attempted to step closer, but Chogan's hand stopped him.

"No, stay out. Restless souls. Something happened here, and you don't want to interfere with things you don't understand. This is for the living." He gestured behind Raul. "Over there is trouble for anyone who doesn't comprehend what they're meddling with. There's a darkness here, an unsettled energy you shouldn't mess with." He pointed to the open field of graves.

"Okay, so what happened here? Who are these people? Who is buried here?"

"Don't know," Chogan said in a low voice, his dark eyes meeting Raul's. "I've been watching this town for over a month now. Something about it just doesn't add up. It doesn't exist on any maps or official records. You're a cop—or were, as you said. How does that happen? Who has the kind of power to make that happen? Which three-letter agency owns this town? You find those answers, and then you'll have a better idea who's buried here."

"So we're talking CIA or FBI? You know that for sure."

Raul already suspected something much deeper, his heart pounding in his chest at the implications.

"More likely an agency no one's heard of, you know, from the black books." Chogan leveled his gaze at Raul as if he were fucking with him or testing him. Raul still wondered what side he was on. "But whoever they are, they're good at hiding their tracks. You were in town. Didn't it strike you as strange how clean, how perfect this place is, as if it's the set of a movie? When actors finish for the day, they go home, but this place, from what I've seen, people who come here…they don't leave."

Raul pulled his hand over his face. "So you think this is, what, a black ops town? I've heard about them, too taboo for anyone to talk about. If this is one, what is the government doing here? You figure it out. A month you've been here, watching, so you did see Wyatt?"

The shadows deepened around them, and the growing darkness mirrored the increasing weight of dread in Raul's chest. He couldn't help but wonder what other secrets this man had seen, and whether he was leading him into a trap. Trust was shaky here.

"As I said, I may have seen him. You understand what kinds of things happen out of sight of the average person who would never be able to grasp this kind of evil. Experiments, training, and likely a lot more than I've been able to make sense of. You may want to consider getting back in your pickup and driving away, forgetting about this place. It would be healthier."

Raul realized Chogan was serious. He let his gaze linger on the unmarked graves. The ominous silence of the forest unsettled him. "You're right," he said. "That would be the smart thing to do, bury my head in the sand and tell myself to forget about this place. Only problem is that I've never done that, especially not when someone fucks around with someone I care about. No, if it's all the same to you, I plan on sticking around, poking around, looking around. You said you've been watching this place for a while, so you're staying around here?"

Chogan said nothing for a moment, then gestured to Raul. "Come on. Best make our way back. We're losing light fast, and you don't want to be out here after dark," was all he said, leaving everything unanswered, as he turned and headed back on the same path. "If you're looking for a place to stay, there's a motel just out of the other side of town," he finally said. "I'm pretty sure it's run by the same people who run this place, but at least it's outside. You want to stay, just watch your back."

He cast an odd look at Raul, and as they walked, Raul couldn't shake the feeling that the shadows were closing in on him, whispering secrets best left undisturbed, hinting at a darkness that lay just beneath the surface. He was more convinced now that whatever Wyatt had stumbled upon, whoever or whatever was running this place hadn't left him alive to talk about it.

CHAPTER 7

Raul squinted against the bright light of what he figured was a hundred-watt bulb outside the door to his motel room as he headed inside. It was a small, dingy place on the outskirts of Shadow Valley, just like Chogan had said, another place he'd never been. It was a basic motel room with a bed, stains on the floor, and a musty odor in the air.

Raul stood in the open doorway. A few doors down, a man leaned against the railing outside, looking down at the darkened parking lot, lit with only one streetlight. The man had short wavy brown hair and freckles, wearing a worn T-shirt and faded blue jeans. He wasn't overweight, but he wasn't that tall and appeared more on the stocky side. Raul realized he was now looking right at him.

"Hey, there," the man called out, pushing himself off the railing and extending a callused hand. "Name's Jeffrey Snider."

Raul left the door open, shoving the key in his pocket, and took a step over and accepted the handshake cautiously. The man was a little too friendly for his liking. "Raul. Just passing through."

"This is quite the slice of paradise. The town, I mean, not this piece of crap." Jeffrey tapped the steel rail with a half-smile, revealing a set of straight white teeth. Raul couldn't shake the feeling that the friendliness of this stranger was off. More than likely, he was from the town.

Before he could say anything, though, he heard footsteps and glanced over his shoulder to see Chogan, who flashed a wide smile. "Finally caught up with you. Was here earlier, but you weren't."

Raul realized Chogan wasn't talking to him. He had walked right past him and over to Jeffrey, whose shoulder he slapped. Apparently, they knew each other. Jeffrey was solid and stocky, about a foot shorter than Chogan.

He didn't remember Chogan mentioning someone else was there, which was odd, considering this was the same motel he'd just told Raul about.

"Raul, this is Jeffrey," Chogan said. "We go way back."

"We just met," Raul said. "Didn't know you knew each other."

Chogan said nothing.

Jeffrey was watching him, now unsmiling. "He on the same page?" was all he said to Chogan, gesturing to Raul, and seemed to hesitate before letting his amber eyes settle on him.

"He's looking into what happened to his friend, who found this place yesterday. Remember the guy in the woods you told me about yesterday, running, before the storm?"

Well, that had Raul's attention. Jeffrey pulled his arms over his broad chest and narrowed his gaze, then gestured out beyond the motel. "I told you the guy was a hunter, yeah. I saw him looking around, and then he was gone. That was your friend? I called out to him, but maybe he didn't hear me."

The knot tightened in Raul's chest. Why hadn't Chogan just told him this instead of playing what felt like a fucking mind game?

"His friend is now dead, found in a motel in another town," Chogan said. "I crossed paths with Raul, here, up at the lookout point the other side of town. Showed him the field."

Jeffrey evidently knew the field, by his grim expression. He winced. "Hey, man, so sorry. You know what happened to your friend?"

He seemed rather chatty, but Raul wasn't too comfortable being there anymore. He looked over the railing, down at his old pickup in the parking lot. A newer crew cab and an older Jeep were parked alongside it. "My friend was found two hundred miles away, dead, in a motel room, but you saw him running? You see someone chasing him? I'm here for answers, but I guess I don't really know why you're here, either of you."

An odd exchange passed again between Jeffrey and Chogan.

"Listen, I only saw him running through the woods, fast," Jeffrey said. "Could have been someone after him, but I didn't see anyone. I'm only a small-town farmer from Pennsylvania. Got a call from my friend, here, about a town that doesn't exist. Chogan insisted on poking around, but the problem is that trouble always seems to follow him, even when he's not looking for it. You going to be trouble for my friend?" Jeffrey moved to take a step toward Raul, ready to fight, but Chogan slapped a hand to his chest.

"Hey, calm down. He's good. Raul's a former cop, just trying to find out what happened to his friend, is all. I watched him drive into town. He says he's not part of this place. I believe him."

What was it about the protective instinct of this farmer from Pennsylvania? Raul still didn't understand what they were doing there.

"Jeffrey and I go way back," Chogan said. "He's always my first call for anything, and he shows up, thinking I need help when I don't."

"Yeah, well, you disappear for too long sometimes," Jeffrey said. "I worry. So you're a cop?"

Raul studied Jeffrey for a moment. He and Chogan were mismatched, complete opposites. "Small-town cop in a few places, but I was a marine first."

"So you're looking into what happened to your friend and who's responsible. From what I've seen the past couple of days I've been here, it isn't going to be easy for you to find out. I may be just a farmer..."

"Yeah, yeah, we get it: Never underestimate the resourcefulness of a farmer," Chogan cut in.

Jeffrey grinned, flexing one bicep for emphasis. "Just saying, I can handle a twelve-gauge and fix just about anything with some duct tape and baling wire."

Raul realized there was more they weren't saying. He looked past the open door to his room, out to the dated and rusty motel sign, its light casting an eerie glow on the chipping paint. He shifted his weight from one foot to another. His stomach rumbled, considering he hadn't eaten a thing since breakfast.

"So Chogan called you here, but I guess I don't understand what you're doing," Raul said, his voice low. He couldn't shake the feeling they were being watched.

"Chogan is like a brother to me," Jeffrey replied, rubbing the back of his neck. "When he told me about this town, I knew I had to come and see it for myself. Poking around has only confirmed what he was saying. But, honestly, I'm just here to convince him to leave well enough alone."

Before Raul could respond, Chogan reached out and tapped his friend's shoulder. "You know I'm not leaving. Something is really wrong here, and I'm going to figure it out. I've got something to look into," he muttered, then walked past Jeffrey down the stairs.

"I'm going to grab my bag." Raul gestured with his thumb, thinking he'd follow Chogan. As he closed the door of his room, he realized Jeffrey was right behind him, and he accompanied him down the concrete stairs. Raul stopped in front of his pickup as the crunch of Chogan's footsteps faded beyond the parking lot.

"You know, Chogan is convinced there's a black op going on here," Raul said, leaning against the hood of his truck, arms folded across his chest. "I mentioned the CIA, but he said it could be something else. So," he continued, searching Jeffrey's eyes for any sign of deceit, "you think he's right?"

Jeffrey let out a heavy sigh, his face creased with worry. "It's hard to put my finger on it. Everything seems perfect on the surface, but towns are never this clean. There's always a drunk or two, some shithead teens dumping trash or kicking a garbage can over, always someone having a bad day, being rude and nasty or distracted on the phone. But what I see here, from a quick look around, is pristine, neat, and tidy. In no normal place is everyone dressed perfectly. I've never before felt as if everyone was watching me the minute I walked into town. I've been told

I see things others don't, but I'm telling you I get the heebie-jeebies here. A darkness is lurking beneath that pretty little town. I swear I've seen men in suits watching from a distance, and I'm not being paranoid."

Raul mulled over Jeffrey's words and found himself glancing into the motel office, remembering the older man who had checked him in. "You see any cameras here? We're, what, maybe five miles from town? Look at this place, old, rundown, but I can't shake the feeling that someone is watching, maybe listening."

Jeffrey stilled and followed his gaze to the office, then behind him to the stairs.

Raul sensed the undercurrent of secrecy, a palpable tension that hung in the air like fog. "Your feelings may be right," he said, "but feelings aren't cold, hard facts, and unfortunately, that's what's needed to prove something bad is happening here and to figure out what Wyatt saw, what scared him, and who killed him."

Jeffrey seemed to consider something, pulling his arms over his chest as his gaze returned to the office. "Do you ever wonder what goes on at night, hidden from the light of day?"

It was an odd comment. "Nothing good, everything bad," Raul said.

"Exactly. You hungry? Because I'm starving. There's a cute little restaurant right at the edge of town. Feel like grabbing a bite?"

He hadn't expected that. In fact, he still wanted to know where Chogan had disappeared to. "Right in the lion's den, huh?" he said. "Yeah, I could eat."

Jeffrey shrugged. "What better way to see what's going on? Or rather, what they want us to see, and maybe what they don't."

Raul stood by his pickup, parked across from the cafe, which had been closing as soon as they walked in. The town square was lit up like a Christmas tree, and Raul shoved his hands in his pockets, feeling the evening chill. The closed sign flicked on in the window of the small corner cafe as Jeffrey, in a brown coat, exited and headed across the street toward him, carrying a takeaway bag.

"They wouldn't do a burger, as they shut the grill off already, but they had some cold chicken and made up a couple sandwiches," Jeffrey called out. "Hope you're not picky."

Raul reached for the sandwich held out to him, wrapped in foil. "That works." He unwrapped it, seeing white bread and lettuce, and took a bite. "It's pretty good. Fills the hole. Thanks for talking them into it."

Jeffrey fell in beside him on the sidewalk. "Seemed more like they were in a hurry to get me out of there. Interesting thing, first time I've seen a cafe that doesn't have any hours. But she did tell me they open at eight for breakfast."

Raul took another bite. They were headed to the square, with a huge gazebo in its center.

"Have you noticed how perfect this town seems?" Jeffrey asked.

Raul hadn't stopped scanning the dark horizon, the buildings around the square, trying to make sense of everything.

"It's like a picture-perfect postcard that never changes."

Raul nodded as he took the last bite of his sandwich and crumpled up the foil, which he tossed into the single garbage can in the idyllic town square. The can was completely empty otherwise. "There's something eerie about this quiet," he agreed. "Almost too perfect to be real."

"Exactly," Jeffrey said, leaning in closer and lowering his voice. "And the people…they're friendly, sure, but they're also secretive. They don't talk much, and when they do, it's in hushed tones. It's as if they're all hiding something."

"Or protecting something," Raul said.

"Right," Jeffrey continued. "I've been doing some exploring, trying to figure out what could be so important, so hidden that everyone's on edge."

"Did you find anything?" Raul wasn't sure why, but he hadn't expected such curiosity from a farmer.

"Maybe," Jeffrey replied hesitantly. "In the woods outside town, there's a place built into the side of a hill, with a steel door and concrete around it. Haven't a clue where it goes or what's inside, but I'm betting it's not good."

Raul hesitated, pulling in a breath. Jeffrey shoved the last of his sandwich in his mouth and crumpled up the foil before tossing it in the garbage too, then wiped his hands together. Raul was remembering Wyatt's voice, his terror at seeing two women with guns at a table outside a door leading to what he had suspected was an underground lab. The similarity to the door in the woods Jeffrey had described had him thinking, but he wasn't about to share his thoughts with someone he'd just met.

"Jeffrey," Raul began cautiously, "you remember where that door is?"

Jeffrey stopped and frowned, then nodded. "I do. It's not far from the field Chogan showed you. Why?"

There was his uneasiness again. "I want to have a look. Can you take me there?"

"Let me guess, you want to get in and see what's going on?" Jeffrey was rather direct as he leaned in.

Raul just stared at the shorter man, wondering how much he'd really want to know. "That's what I do, and if it gives me the answers I'm looking for, it's a place to start. There's no telling what I'll find there, where it goes, what's inside. Just tell me where it is. I'll drive you back to the motel."

"You're going to go there in the dark, tonight?" His voice was deep, sharp.

Raul found himself looking around to see if anyone was listening. "The dark of night is always better because that's when people are sleeping. I know what I'm doing. I would really like to have a look around, and I'd prefer to have less eyes on me."

Jeffrey pulled his cell out of his pocket and stared at the screen. "Chogan is wondering where we are."

Raul hadn't even heard the text come in. There were a lot of secrets between Chogan and Jeffrey, who they were and why they were really there. So much about them he couldn't figure out. A cool wind had whipped up. "I'd like to know where he went, too."

Jeffrey smirked as he texted something. "I stopped asking that exact thing of Chogan because he becomes so damn vague when he doesn't want to tell you something. That's why I'm here in a place I'd rather not be. I have a good life, you know, but here I am in the middle of nowhere, in a town that doesn't exist, with a bunch of people who are part of something I probably have no idea about, and I guarantee you I don't want to know." The screen flashed with the reply before he shoved it in his pocket again. "Chogan should be here any minute. It seems he's already back in town. You want to see this secret door? I'll take you. You said your friend is dead, so I figure we can at least watch your back."

Raul hadn't expected that. He had to remind himself this would be easier with a little help. "It could be dangerous," he said. "You may want to sit it out."

Jeffrey pulled up the zipper of his coat. "If I want to sit anything out, I'll go home where I'm safer and warmer. We'll wait for Chogan, and I'll take you. You know, I don't know you, but for some reason Chogan likes you. I've known Chogan forever, and he doesn't like or trust just anyone."

Raul didn't know what to make of that. As they waited for Chogan, the lights in the cafe went out, and a woman stepped out and locked the door behind her. "You know," Raul said, "one of the things I've learned is that there's always a weak link, someone who will talk. You just get a feeling for it. Maybe someone's scared about saving their own skin, or something has gone one step too far and their conscience has gotten the better of them."

Jeffrey turned, also watching the lady in a red coat as she walked around the corner of the building and disappeared. "You talking about her?"

Raul shrugged. "Her or someone else. Keep poking, keep asking…"

A rustle of leaves, and Raul turned to see Chogan emerge from the wooded path leading into town. The man's ebony hair was tied back in its usual ponytail, and he still wore his faded blue coat, his hands shoved in his pockets, scanning the surroundings with practiced caution.

"You two look cozy." Chogan's voice was low. Raul

didn't know him well enough to tell whether he was serious.

"I was telling Raul about the door that appears out of the side of the hill. He wants me to show him."

Chogan stopped, letting his gaze linger a second on Raul before looking away as if scanning the area. "Who drove?"

"I did," Raul said.

All Chogan said in reply was, "Well, let's go."

It took Raul a second to understand what he was saying and what he wasn't.

"Okay," he said. He wanted to laugh, and he probably would have if everything about the situation hadn't been so dire. Chogan was already walking, and Raul fell in behind with Jeffrey as they headed back across the square to his pickup, still parked at the curb across from the cafe. Raul wasn't sure what made him look, but as he walked around to the driver's side and pulled open the door, he spotted who he realized was the police chief leaning against his car half a block down, watching them.

CHAPTER 8

"Y'all notice the chief watching us?" Raul broke the silence that had settled in the truck as he gripped the steering wheel, driving his old pickup out of town on the darkened road. He turned down the same pullout he had parked at earlier, then flipped off his lights as he proceeded just into the trail in the trees, out of sight from anyone who might be looking, and shut off the engine. He glanced at Jeffrey, sitting between him and Chogan, who was riding shotgun. With three big men in the pickup, there wasn't a lot of room left.

"Yeah, I noticed him," replied Chogan, then only grunted as he opened the passenger door and stepped out.

Jeffrey glanced over at Chogan and then back at Raul, who had followed suit, opening his door as quietly as he could. He walked around the back of the truck.

"He's got his eye on all of us—on you, on me," Chogan continued unexpectedly. "That guy is some kind of watcher for the town. What do you want to bet that right now, they're going through your motel room? They'll plant bugs so they can keep track of what you're doing, what you're saying, watching everything you do."

Raul rested his hand on his truck bed. "That's exactly what I would do. If he has his eye on us, it would be prudent for us to keep closer tabs on him. Maybe I'll drive in and pay him a visit tomorrow."

"And say what?" Jeffrey said, closing the passenger door.

Raul reached into the back of his pickup, lifted the truck bed cover, and pulled out a flashlight. "No idea, but I'm quick on my feet. I'll just see where it goes." He flicked on the flashlight and handed it to Jeffrey, who was now beside him. Chogan was already walking toward the trail in the dark. Raul reached for another flashlight, flicked it on, and followed the two down the same trail from earlier that day.

"If it's all the same to you, I'd rather not be out here too long," Jeffrey said. "Let's get moving. In and out."

As the two fell in behind him, Raul had a feeling Chogan knew more about what was going on than he was letting on.

Jeffrey kept looking over his shoulder at Raul. "So have you thought about what you're going to do? Because I have to tell you, I'm fast feeling we could be in over our heads."

"Hey, cut it out," Chogan snapped. "You're too noisy back there. Stop talking. The last thing I want to be doing is announcing ourselves." He had stopped, his voice low, eyes darting from Raul to Jeffrey, whom he tapped on his chest with the back of his hand. "I told you to go home. You don't need to stay, but I do."

Raul couldn't help but speculate about the relationship between Chogan and Jeffrey. They seemed unusually close, yet such opposites. Something about the way Chogan had stressed his need to stay had Raul wondering whether there was something personal about this town to him. Chogan had already headed down an embankment, considerably familiar with the terrain.

"Tell me what it is about this place that has Chogan poking around," Raul said quietly to Jeffrey. "I know my reason but not his."

Jeffrey hadn't moved. When he turned around, his expression was hard, unreadable. "Chogan always has a reason; he just doesn't always share it," he said, then followed his friend down.

That absurd comment was beyond cryptic, and Raul couldn't imagine what, exactly, it meant as he followed again, walking in silence in the dark of night. The forest was quiet, unnerving, yet it held the potential for an unshakeable disturbance.

Raul let his flashlight shine over the field of the dead as Chogan paused for a moment.

"This is spooky as shit," Jeffrey said.

"Let's go," Chogan returned in a low voice as he headed around the field and down a short path.

As soon as he stopped and raised his hand, a chill passed over Raul, who frantically glanced behind himself, uncertain of what he was supposed to be looking out for.

Chogan shone his flashlight on his face, revealing an expression that was anything but friendly. "We should be getting close," he said, "so watch your step and look out for anything that sticks out." But before they could move forward, he turned back to them. "Did either of you stop to think why something like this is out here, in the middle of nowhere? This town, this place—you find a door in the woods, and I can tell you, ninety-nine percent of the time it leads deep underground. There are tunnels everywhere, yet no one ever asks why."

Though Raul hadn't expected such an existential thought from Chogan, he found himself nodding in agreement. He took a deep breath against the rising fear that had become an unwelcome friend. "I figured as much already," he said. "Tunnels everywhere, yet no one seems to know what's underneath their feet. You know what? Let's get going."

Chogan started walking again. The trail was narrow, the bushes thick. If anyone was out there listening, they would have heard them coming. "Here it is, just behind this shrubbery. You'd keep walking if you didn't know it was there. But once you see it, you can't miss it."

Raul shone his flashlight over the concrete behind the bush that Chogan had walked around. There was a steel door with a deadbolt and what looked like a keypad. Definitely out of place, from what he could see in the dark, as if built right into the side of the hill. Chogan was already at the door, turning the knob, but it didn't open.

"It's locked," Jeffrey said from behind them. "I guess that's enough for me. We should get back."

Raul glanced back at the short, stocky man. He was the weaker link and way out of his element.

Chogan pulled something from his pocket and said, "Shine the light over here." He had already squatted down and shoved a pick into the lock.

"Hey, hey, what are you doing?" Jeffrey said in a low voice, rather sharply, in a near panic. "You want to go in? Because I don't. We were just supposed to come here, show him, that's it. Not go in. Are you crazy?"

Chogan picked the lock with skill, like a locksmith. There was a click, and he stood up and pulled the door open a crack. "Well, you can wait out here if you want," he said. "Keep an eye out for us."

Raul looked past Chogan down the concrete tunnel that stretched out before them. Its sterile lighting did little to quell the foreboding that hung heavy in the air. Unease emanated from Jeffrey, a mixture of frustration, anger, and fear etched into his expression. Even in the darkness, it seemed as though he had paled.

"Yeah, no, I'm not waiting out here," he said. "Pretty sure I've seen enough movies to know that the dumbass who waits outside as the lookout is the first one taken out." He stepped determinedly past Raul and followed Chogan inside, leaving the dark forest behind.

Raul hesitated only for a moment, glancing back into the darkness and flicking off his flashlight. He tucked it in his pocket and followed, closing the door quietly behind them. The well-lit concrete tunnel in which the trio now stood was a stark contrast to the shadowy woods outside.

As they walked deeper, into the belly of the beast, the tension grew, and Raul couldn't shake the feeling that they were entering a different world. It was too easy to continue walking forward, guided by the intrigue of the unknown, to whatever hidden danger awaited them. An eerie silence prevailed, leaving Raul again with that unsettled sense of being trapped. It was a feeling he couldn't shake.

Finally, they reached the end of the corridor and were confronted by two paths—one to the left, the other to the right, each through a separate door. Chogan's hand rested on the door to the right, and he cast a meaningful glance back at Jeffrey and Raul. No one said a word as he opened the door and led them into a vast, dimly lit room.

Jeffrey swore under his breath as he stepped inside.

"Quiet," was all Chogan said in a whisper over his shoulder as Raul held the door.

The room was dominated by a massive glass wall that looked down into a sprawling laboratory. People in white coats bustled about, their movements deliberate and precise. Beds built into the walls held unconscious figures, unsettlingly still.

"Holy shit, what the hell is this?" Jeffrey muttered, his voice barely above a whisper.

Raul took another step closer to the glass, his eyes darting around the room, taking in the chairs, desks, computer equipment, and cameras, all shrouded in darkness. Oddly, no one was there in the observation point where they stood, as if it had been shut down for the night. He expected the glass was tinted, maybe one-way only. The silence that lingered was unnerving.

"How many are there?" Jeffrey's voice trembled, but Raul's attention was drawn elsewhere. His heart pounded as he recognized a familiar face among the slumbering figures—a light-haired woman with narrowed eyes and a slender nose. Lydia. His brother's wife. No, this couldn't be possible. He couldn't look away, not even when he felt a hand on his arm. Chogan was right there, watching him closely.

"What is it?" he said. "You look like you've seen a ghost."

Raul gave his head a shake, searching out Lydia again, wondering whether his eyes were playing tricks on him. But it was her. He said nothing as he looked at all the resting people, men on one side, women on the other.

"Third from the end, that's my brother's wife," Raul said quietly, the implications of her presence sinking in. He couldn't look away. "My brother has it all wrong. He's not even looking for her. No one is. How? Why? He thinks Lydia walked out on him with the kids. Five kids. Oh, my Lord, how is this possible?"

Chogan watched him sadly. "The question is how did she get here? Was she taken forcibly, or did she just wander in accidentally?"

Raul wanted to yell, pound the glass, but he did none of that.

"You think the kids are here too?" Jeffrey asked.

All Raul could do was shake his head. "Maybe. They have to be," he said.

As he stared down at her sleeping body, the idea of what the hell they had put her through in this place sickened him. It wasn't just answers about Wyatt he was searching for now. He needed to figure out a way to get Lydia out of there and then find his brother's kids.

CHAPTER 9

The late morning sun was hidden by thick clouds, casting eerie shadows on the streets of the small town. A palpable sense of unease hung heavy in the air, like a shroud that refused to lift, but that was likely from staring at the dingy motel room ceiling. Raul had been unable to shut his eyes during the few hours he'd tried to sleep. He knew all too well that something was terribly wrong. The discovery of Lydia, his brother's wife, in that secret lab as a victim of some twisted experiment had sent a chill down his spine. It had killed him to leave, but Chogan had been right. The only way to save her was to figure out what they were up against.

Right now, he knew jack shit. Every step he'd taken on that trail, he'd gone over and over in his mind. Adding to that, he couldn't shake the feeling that he was being watched every second of his waking life, and the knowledge that his motel room was likely bugged with audio and video surveillance only deepened his paranoia.

As Raul walked down the motel stairs, he spotted a young man leaning against the wall of the brick building.

It was Jeffrey he saw next, speaking to the man, whose straight blond hair shimmered in the faded sunlight.

"There you are," Jeffrey said. "I was about to knock on your door. This is Robin Fox." He gestured to the man, who was slender and about five foot seven, he thought, with blue eyes that stared at him intently. He didn't know why, but he picked up on a feminine quality.

But Raul really wasn't in the mood to meet anyone. All he did was nod, saying, "Robin, nice to meet you," then let his gaze linger on Jeffrey.

"Robin is a fourth-year med student," Jeffrey said.

Robin pulled his arms over his chest and cut in, "Yes, was, past tense. I'm currently suspended for my character flaw of having a rebellious nature and a further willingness to challenge any and all authority. That doesn't work in the field of medicine, as I've found out." His appearance belied a steely determination that Raul found intriguing, or maybe it was the fact that he was so unapologetic.

"Explain to Raul what you told me," Jeffrey said.

Raul wondered if it was the lack of sleep that was making him so uneasy. "What is this about?" he said, his tone guarded. He glanced around to ensure they weren't drawing unwanted attention, knowing they were likely being watched closely.

"Your friend," Robin said, "was telling me about your brother's wife, Lydia, and everything else that's happening in this town."

Raul let his gaze settle hard on Jeffrey, wondering whether he was just plain stupid or trying to get them killed. "Oh, and what else did my friend say?" he replied, more a warning than a question.

Jeffrey held both hands up as if to calm him. "It's not

like that. Robin has been looking into this place, too. He already discovered the underground lab we found last night. There are more who have stumbled on this place just like your friend Wyatt did."

Robin turned, glancing over his shoulder, and then ran a hand through his hair. Frustration was etched into his face. "I've been digging into things here, and I think I'm starting to see the bigger picture. You know you're being watched?"

Jeffrey was nodding. Raul wanted to pull him aside and ask if he had lost his mind, but he was stuck on the phrase 'being watched,' which had confirmed his suspicions.

"Yeah, I can see by your face that you don't trust me," Robin said. "Why would you? You don't know me, just like I don't know you. Another of my many faults is that I'm not afraid to stand up to those in power, even if it costs me everything. There are more of us looking into things and the people here."

Raul stared at Robin for a moment, considering his words. "All right," he said finally, his voice low and steady, wondering if he was being played. "Let's talk. Tell me what you know, but not here."

Raul wasn't sure what made him look away from Robin then, but he spotted a woman with dark hair striding across the motel parking lot toward them. She walked determinedly, looking to the side, her hands shoved in her jacket pockets. She wasn't very tall. Close behind her was a man with red hair and heavy freckles, chewing gum, about Raul's height but with an extra thirty pounds.

"You know these two?" Raul muttered to Jeffrey, his gaze never leaving the approaching pair.

"Met them earlier. Harley Ray and Duke Dunlop," Jeffrey replied, keeping his voice low.

"You want to know what I know?" Robin said, his blue eyes conveying his familiarity with the approaching duo. "These two are who you want to talk to. They're here to help."

"And they're not from the town, are they?" Raul said.

"No, not from here."

"Who's this?" the dark-haired woman asked as she approached, looking right at Raul, likely with the same suspicion he had for her.

"This is Raul Booth, a friend of Jeffrey's. He stumbled in yesterday. Bad news, too—his friend is dead because of something he saw here, and his brother's wife is in that lab they found underground last night."

Everyone was quiet, and Raul felt so damn uncomfortable. He turned to Jeffrey. "Seriously? I don't know these people," he said, keeping his voice low.

Jeffrey was already shaking his head. "Relax. They already know Chogan. Harley Ray is former CIA."

The woman, Harley, wasn't smiling as Jeffrey gestured to her. The red-headed man, however, held out his hand to Raul.

"Hey, I get what you mean," he said. "The name's Duke Dunlop. I'm a journalist, or was. Every story I try to write gets tanked because my only interest is exposing corruption in government, missing tax dollars, and secret programs. As my last editor advised, that's what will eventually have me on a slab in the morgue or in hiding. So when Robin called about this place, I was already here."

Raul shook his hand, which was large and warm. Duke's blue eyes seemed hard, cold, and Raul suspected he had a bit of a temper, too.

Duke gestured to the woman. "Harley and I go way back. She was my second call, considering spook shit is her MO."

"You know there are some things I can't talk about," Harley said, her hands still in her brown leather jacket pockets. She wore blue jeans, and he thought he saw her gun holstered inside. He was stuck on the idea of her having been in the CIA, wondering what her story was.

Raul nodded. "Sedition or treason, is it? They can come after you with guns blazing."

She was looking right at him, her eyes light brown, as was her face. A pretty woman who could kick some serious butt, he figured. "That's how they keep their secrets, the deep state, the shadow government. When you see, you can't unsee."

"Okay, so how are you helping if you can't talk?" Jeffrey asked.

Duke smiled oddly as he glanced over at Harley. "I would think her covert skills and knowledge of inside information might help. So tell me, Harley, what is this place? I suspect you already have some idea of what's going on here."

"Cut to the chase. I like that," Harley said, her eyes locking on to Raul with an intensity that made him shift uncomfortably. "I have my suspicions, but being a spy doesn't mean I know everything. Anyone ever hear about CIA towns?"

"We're talking spook shit again, aren't we?" Robin cut in, no longer leaning against the motel wall.

Raul found himself looking over his shoulder to see if anyone else was around.

"Let me tell you a story," Harley said. "Imagine places in the middle of nowhere, with no government oversight, where experiments can be conducted and secret programs can operate on unsuspecting people. Scenarios could even be practiced in preparation for an event."

Raul knew he was frowning again. She was talking around whatever she couldn't say. His gaze shifted between her and Duke, who was chewing gum incessantly. "What kind of event? Are we talking about a false flag or something else?" he said, his voice low and cautious. Did she already know something of the scenario in the works for this town? "To be clear," he continued, "I don't know you and I don't trust you."

"I just told you a story," Harley replied rather sharply. "I never said there would be an event."

"Kids, be nice," Duke jumped in. "Okay, now that we've established our mutual distrust, how about we discuss what brought us here? Raul, you start."

He said nothing for a moment, then took a deep breath. "Got a call from a childhood friend, Wyatt. He stumbled upon this place, called me, freaked out, spouting weird shit about experiments. He was on his way back home but never showed. Then got a call from a detective the next morning, saying he was found dead in a motel room two hundred miles away," Raul said, his jaw clenched so tight it ached. "Evidently, Jeffrey told you about the lab. My brother's wife was there, yeah, with others. The thing is, I didn't know she was missing. My brother said she left him and took their kids. He hasn't heard from her, so I'm thinking someone or something brought her here. Then there are the kids, five of them. If she's here, where are they? What kind of experiments are these people doing?"

Something in Duke's expression softened, with sympathy, maybe. Then he shook his head. "I've been investigating unexplained financial transactions, missing persons, and rumors of a powerful group pulling the strings. When Robin called me about this town, I did some looking, but I can tell you I didn't expect anything as sophisticated as this. You drive in here, and it's like the perfect suburbia. You feel the eyes on you; I guarantee everyone here is in on whatever's going on…"

"Spooks like me don't end up in small towns by accident, either," Harley cut in, her tone clipped. "My gut told me there was more to this place than met the eye. I have contacts, I know how to stay under the radar, and I know how to dig up dirt when I need to. At the same time, I know when something can get me killed."

"Seems like we're all here for a reason," Jeffrey chimed in, rubbing the back of his neck thoughtfully. "Maybe it's not just a coincidence."

"Maybe not," Robin, who had been so quiet, finally cut in. "You know, one of the first things I learned in medical school is to shut up and listen. But following orders and doing as I'm told never sat right with me. So I've sat back and listened a lot, and one thing I know well is that even though experimentation is how we make advances, sometimes experiments cross the line. Sometimes experiments are done in secret because they go outside the bounds of acceptability and step more into the gray area of psychotic. Torturing a human, a child, an animal, it takes a special breed, if you know what I mean. If anything, we need to be careful. As you said, Raul, we're being watched. Now, I'm not a spook, but I think we need to find a new place to meet and come up with a better cover story."

Raul took a second to consider who these people were, a journalist, a med student, a spook. They definitely could help if they were who they said.

"Unexplained disappearances," Robin continued, his

voice low and urgent. "That's what drew me here. A friend's sister, who is as stable as they come, vanished. Here I am, and all I've found is people vanishing without a trace, with no explanation from the authorities. I followed a crumb, I still don't know how, and stumbled upon a place that doesn't exist on any map. You remember my call to you, Harley, when I asked you how a town can exist in real life but not on paper? Your silence said everything."

Harley was staring intently at Robin. Raul figured there had to be a story behind how they knew each other. She pulled her arms defiantly over her chest. "As I said, there are things I can't and won't talk about. But what I can talk about are the things here that don't add up. Inexplicable noises, unmarked vehicles with tinted windows, and cryptic messages on social media that I stumbled across."

"It's too perfect," Duke chimed in, really working his piece of gum. "This town has a way of covering things up. Makes you think everything's fine, the perfect place, but no place is ever perfect."

Jeffrey was taking all of them in, seeming rather tight-lipped all of a sudden.

Raul pulled his hand from his pocket and tapped him on the chest. "Where's Chogan?"

Jeffrey took a deep breath. "He was gone when I got up, but then, at times I think he doesn't sleep," he said, which made Raul think there was more to Chogan than he realized.

"Pretty sure I saw him having coffee this morning at that coffeehouse with the lady who runs it," Duke said. Raul hadn't realized he even knew Chogan. There was something curious in the blue eyes of the reporter staring back at him. Duke shrugged. "When I spotted him, he pretended not to know me, so I figured he was working some angle. I've never met anyone who can read people better than he can and get them talking, and that lady is a talker."

Raul let his gaze linger for a second, taking in Harley, Robin, and then Jeffrey. "So you all know each other? How'd you all meet? I mean, I know this guy's story..." He gestured to Jeffrey, then glanced between the other three, who exchanged an odd look.

"Chogan and I are friends," Jeffrey jumped in before anyone could answer, then shrugged. "We only met Robin the other day. Just saying, in this shitshow, it's nice to have more eyes on this place than just ours."

"Duke and I were college roommates," Robin said, "and Harley was the girl who broke my heart."

Harley was watching him intently, as if trying to figure him out. "Your heart wasn't broken," she said, "because we never were and were never going to be an item. We were and still are friends, and the three of us never drifted apart."

Raul didn't know what to make of the soft chuckle from Duke, whose amusement seemed to lighten a rather dark situation. Harley had crossed her arms over her chest, and the way she stared at him was filled with an unapologetic challenge, one he wasn't about to accept.

"You know what?" he said. "I think it's time I had a sit-down with the police chief, feel him out."

"I'll go with you," Harley cut in unexpectedly. "You drive," she said to Raul, then tapped Duke's arm. "You see if that library is open. You two can check out some of the shops in town and see what you can observe. We'll meet up later."

Raul wondered whether he frowned. The woman seemed to be handling all of them, becoming the self-appointed leader, and everyone seemed fine with that. At last, she gestured to him, and she and he headed in the direction of his pickup as Jeffrey, Duke, and Robin all went the other way.

Raul couldn't help but think to himself that no matter how much he had just learned about this woman, young and attractive, there was still so much he had yet to figure out. After all, the only thing he knew about spooks was that one couldn't trust them.

CHAPTER 10

Raul and Harley stepped into the police chief's office, the door creaking loudly as it opened. The chief sat behind an unusually neat and tidy desk, sipping coffee from a stained mug. He looked up, and the way he tracked them, his eyes narrowing beneath the brim of a faded ball cap, would have likely scared a lesser man, Raul figured.

"Can I help you?" he asked gruffly, setting down his mug with a thud that echoed in the otherwise quiet room. Neat, tidy, organized, not something Raul had ever associated with any police station.

"Actually," Raul began, his voice steady despite his growing suspicion, "we wanted to ask you a few questions about this town."

"Questions?" The chief leaned back in his chair, crossing his arms over his chest. "Why are you still in my town, Mr. Booth? Last I remember, I was clear with you; this is a closed town. If you're sticking around, you need to register at the town hall, and I know you haven't. You a smart-ass, there?"

He realized it wasn't really a question. The way the chief addressed him had caught him off guard. He glanced at Harley. A subtle look had passed between her and the chief, brief but enough to set Raul on edge again. "If I recall," he said, "you said I need to register if I'm taking up residence, which, I assure you, I'm not. Let's just save each other some time, since I'm pretty sure you already know where I'm staying, in that roadside motel out of town. It wouldn't surprise me if you knew my room number, too, and have already gone through my things. That's outside even your authority, but I get the feeling this entire town is outside every authority. I haven't really figured out how this pretty little place stays this way. Clean, neat, and no one causing trouble? Tell me, what's your secret, Chief?"

The way the chief was staring at him, his eyes reminded him of smoke and mirrors. "Cards on the table? Rules are what make a town a safe, clean place, and you know you've already disobeyed one of many, you and your two cohorts last night. No one, and I mean no one, is to be in the town square after nine p.m." He tsked, again leveling Raul with a look that made him uneasy. He wasn't so stupid as to forget that this man could jam him up or make him suddenly disappear.

"Yes, we saw you watching us. You'd have seen my friend grabbing us a bite to eat and then us leaving town," Raul continued, trying to maintain his composure, wondering how much the man knew.

"I run a tight ship, so to speak, in my town. Just because I'm feeling myself in a good mood, I'm going to give you a second warning. No pickup trucks allowed in town after nine. Now, you go register at the town hall, stating all your business here. Those sidearms you're carrying? You're going to hand them over. There's no unauthorized carrying of any weapons within the town borders without approval, and I don't recall you asking for permission." He gestured to Raul's jacket, under which his sidearm was fastened to his jeans waistband. He evidently had an eye and had seen the bulge.

"Oh, I have a permit," Raul said. "Like you do, Chief. I'm a former law enforcement officer and a military vet. Is this where I need to ask your permission? Because I'm not handing over my gun. As you said, the rules apply within your town, but I'm not staying in your town. I'm here only to ask you a few questions."

Chief Walker was looking only at him, which Raul thought was odd. He found himself glancing back at Harley, who was standing off to the side, by a cabinet and a fax machine. Why was the chief ignoring her?

"Is this about your missing friend?" the chief said. "What was his name again, Wyatt? You want to file a missing person report? Is that why you insist on being here?" He made no move to stand up, open a drawer, or take his eyes off Raul.

"What I want is to know why this town doesn't exist on any map," Raul said. "Why is it so clean? What's really going on here? Everything here, the storefronts, the buildings, the town square, looks as if it was built at the same time, which is impossible. That's one of the tiny details I haven't missed. I can't seem to find any records of the town's incorporation, either. How deep should I dig?"

The chief seemed to grin. Raul wondered whether it was his lack of sleep that had him poking at this man, who was the eyes, ears, and muscle of an amoral style of law and order that Raul had seen too often. "Yes, you have quite an eye for details, don't you?" the chief said, that slight smile still tugging at his lips. "You know what the problem with this country is? Too many people don't take any pride in their community. Maybe that's what your problem is, too. You're used to seeing chaos, so you've got the wrong idea about this place. It's not a secret or anything like that. We have us a peaceful, quiet community away from the hustle and bustle. I guess it's fortunate for us that it's missing from the maps. It keeps the looky-loos away. As I said, we have rules that are strictly enforced to keep everyone safe and sound and happy, and we take care of our own by keeping an eye out for each other. If something happens, we take action right away to make sure it doesn't become a larger issue. Taking pride means keeping everything looking new."

He leaned forward again, resting his arms on the desk as he looked directly into Raul's eyes. "What we don't like is outsiders. We have our way of doing things, and you coming in here, questioning who we are, trying to imply that something is going on here, well, we don't tolerate such crazy notions. Again, you've been warned. We have rules, and if we know someone isn't going to abide by those rules or may bring trouble upon us," he continued sharply, "we make sure they leave as soon as possible." He paused before adding, "So my question to you, Raul Booth, is are you a troublemaker, and do we need to see that you find your way out of here?"

Raul knew he was toeing the line. No, he'd stepped right over it. "My friend Wyatt saw some things here that didn't make a lick of sense to me. It sounded crazy: experiments, unexplained situations, blacked-out windows of buses. He told me, and maybe I've told someone else."

"Can't quite figure out if you're just plain stupid or a

born troublemaker," the chief said, leaning forward now, both hands flat on the dark wood of the desk, ready to stand. "You're asking questions you don't want answers to, boy. You'd do well to leave now and forget you ever came here."

"Is that a threat?" Raul fired back, his anger rising.

"Consider it a warning." The chief's voice was low and dangerous. "People who poke around where they shouldn't end up regretting it. We run a tight ship here. Everyone knows their place. Crazy talk and stirring up trouble is something I won't allow. Your friend sounds like he's a little crazy, saying the kinds of things no one would believe."

"Except you haven't answered our questions," Raul persisted, feeling as though he was walking a thin line between bravery and foolishness, and the latter might mean taking a bullet in the back of the head.

"Full name and address," the chief barked suddenly, pulling out a pen and a notepad from his top desk drawer. "You were a cop, where, and who in the military did you report to? I'll be doing some checking on you."

Before Raul could respond, Harley tapped him on the chest with the back of her hand as she stepped into his line of sight. The chief was interested only in him, having said nothing to her. "Time to go," she murmured in a low voice, pulling him away from the desk and toward the door.

They stepped out onto the street, the sunlight momentarily blinding them, and he looked back through the window, seeing the chief watching him. Raul glanced down at Harley, his frustration simmering just below the surface. "We didn't learn anything," he snapped. "He's hiding something. Why is it that he was focused only on me? He said nothing to you, as if you know each other. Am I being fucked with, Harley?"

She made a face, looking away. "You went in there all warrior, pushing all his buttons, accusing, challenging, and pushing too hard, which will only put a target on our backs. Of course he wasn't interested in me; I was a shadow in the background." Her eyes scanned their surroundings as if she expected danger to materialize at any moment. "We need to be careful. *You* need to be careful."

"Careful?" Raul scoffed. "We came here for answers, not to tiptoe around some corrupt cop and whatever secret agency is operating out of this place."

"Believe it or not, we did learn something." Harley's voice was low, urgent. "While you were talking to him, I noticed there were no files, no mess, no one else in that office—just a fax machine and a note telling the chief the hunting party is a go for tonight."

"Hunting? Hunting what? Is that code for something?" Raul couldn't shake the sick feeling that things were about to go sideways.

"Could be code for a lot of things. He's not a cop, not in the traditional sense. Law is what you say it is, and this place has its enforcers. They ensure you and I, and everyone else who happens upon it, either move on or disappear. Let's head up to the coffeehouse," she suggested, nodding toward where Duke and Robin sat outside, sipping their drinks. "Maybe they've found something. Might I suggest it may also be prudent for us to watch each other's backs?"

He considered her warning and fell in beside her, heading toward the coffeehouse and feeling the eyes of the community on them. "You think someone's coming for us."

She glanced over to the town square, where the chief was now crossing the road to join a handful of people standing in the middle, talking. "Coming for us, hunting us, disappearing us, or all of the above. Just think about it. What would it take to get rid of your friend and dump him in a motel two hundred miles away?"

He looked down at her, realizing she was smart in a way that should have terrified him. "A well-coordinated effort, I would think."

Harley reached for a pair of sunglasses from her pocket and shoved them on, even though the day was cloudy, before glancing his way, not missing a step. "And then some. You would need to have people everywhere to make it happen. Make a call, get your team ready, kind of like what we're seeing here. So a word of advice, Raul? I get your angst, with a sister-in-law in trouble and a dead friend. But don't go poking the bear. That chief may not be the head of this whole fantasyland, but he's definitely someone who can cause you a world of trouble."

He understood what she was saying, yet time wasn't on their side. "Trouble is no stranger to me."

"Raul, I'm serious. It's a damn miracle you still have your gun." This time, she sounded genuinely pissed.

"Fine, I hear you. Now how about we find out whether anyone has learned anything?"

She made a rude sound under her breath but kept walking. Duke, who sat with Robin, had spotted them and lifted his hand in a wave. Raul's attention, however, was drawn to the chief, still making his way into the town square and over to four older men, every one of whom was now watching them intently, a silent threat hanging in the air like a storm ready to break.

CHAPTER 11

The coffee shop door was propped open, but the hum of the espresso machine drowned out the voices inside as Raul and Harley approached. The outdoor table where Robin and Duke sat seemed a mirage of normalcy on the edge of an unfathomable mystery. Inside, through the broad window, Raul watched Jeffrey, who leaned on the counter, apparently flirting with Deb, the coffee lady.

"Anything?" Raul asked as he pulled out a chair, the metal legs scraping across the concrete.

"Town council was tight-lipped. A couple of women there just handed us a form and pointed to a sign on the wall that said all newcomers must register," Duke replied, his angular face hardening with suspicion. "Didn't, in case you're asking. Pointed out to the one old lady who seemed in charge that we weren't staying, just passing through. The younger one—pretty, Robin couldn't keep his eyes off her—asked us where we were heading."

"She was a looker, what can I say? I like looking at blond, attractive, and sassy women," Robin cut in. "I guarantee you they all know about us already, but Duke told them we're taking the backroads on the long way to St. Louis to see places that aren't on the maps. The shopkeepers, they said they're closed, but as soon as we walked in, it seemed they were expecting us. That illusion, the mom and pop shop, the smile, the welcome. If we didn't already suspect this was a shady town… Heard all the wonderful stuff, that it's a nice community, but the only strangers here are us. Look around. We're being watched. I get the feeling they're scared."

"Scared of what?" Harley piped in, the worry lines around her eyes deepening. It was the first time Raul had noticed how pretty her brown eyes were, and that her face was free of makeup.

"This place, whatever they're part of, or the fact that we're here, sniffing around and about to expose whatever secrets they have. That's enough to scare anyone who's doing something they shouldn't," Duke said, then lifted his paper cup and took a swallow. "Have to say, though, they make better coffee here than I've had anywhere."

"We need to talk to Chogan. He'll know," Robin muttered, fidgeting with his cup and appearing on edge. Raul watched as the man himself, dressed casually in blue jeans, his long dark hair hanging loose, walked up the sidewalk toward them.

Raul nodded at him. "Speak of the devil."

"Kids," Chogan said in a low voice, bluntly, without preamble. "In the woods. About ten of them, led to that same lab we saw last night."

It took Raul a moment to understand, and then that sick feeling settled in the pit of his stomach. "Jesus." He pulled his cell phone from his pocket and thumbed through the photos, pausing on the only one he had of his brother's family at Christmas two years earlier. He held the phone up to Chogan. "We saw Lydia last night. My brother's kids—are they…?" He needed him to say no, but at the same time, he prayed it had been them.

"Couldn't say." Chogan shrugged, his dark eyes revealing nothing more. "They were barefoot, following a woman. Looked like a twisted field trip. Maybe it was innocent; maybe it wasn't."

"Something's happening tonight. They mentioned a hunting party," Robin cut in.

Chogan looked at him sharply. "Hunting what?" he said, taking all of them in and then letting his gaze settle on Raul as if he had all the answers.

"Well, that's the million-dollar question," Raul said. "But my friend Wyatt is dead, and the answers I came here for have changed. Lydia and the kids are all that matter right now. We need to get back in that lab, figure out where they keep everyone."

"You have no fucking idea what we'd be walking into," Harley said, but she wouldn't look at him. "If you want to get her and find the kids, we need to know more, and right now, we know less than nothing."

"What do you suggest, then? Come on, I'm all ears," Raul said, but stopped himself before he could continue, feeling the burn of his words, knowing his emotions and anger always clouded his judgement.

Harley leaned forward, pressing her lips together firmly. She reminded him so much of the spooks he knew and had worked with. They held on to so much, the secrets they knew and wouldn't share. He realized they could never be trusted.

"Have any of you really considered what's going on here?" she said. "Because as we've been sitting here and the puzzle pieces have started to fall together, we may be overthinking it. What if this is a CIA town, you know, where spooks go to learn to survive? They learn torture techniques no one would ever believe exist. The training processes spies go through are nontypical; think crisis actors in a big old make-believe scenario." She pressed her lips together with a subtle glance to the side. "Look around. Doesn't this town look like a movie set? There are CIA museums, too, that are never accessible to the public, that hold all kinds of classified items and artifacts going way back. Behind closed doors, there are so many secrets. I'm thinking mind-control experiments using drugs, hypnosis, trauma, electronic devices, technology you wouldn't believe exists. The lab you found, I'm betting this place would be entirely black-book funded. And all of this is top secret, so secret no one would ever believe you. Don't forget the CIA is known for its complete mystery. Then there's this hunting party. I've been letting it sit, and the only thing that keeps coming to me is human hunting."

No one said anything. Raul wondered what she'd seen.

"You're talking MK Ultra," he said.

Her dark eyes finally locked on to him. "One of many such experiments. The agency continues to experiment on humans and animals using drugs, hypnosis, and electronic devices, but because it's illegal, it's done away from the public. How many people go missing and are never found? Think about it. Your brother's wife is here. How did that happen? Her kids, all those kids, and how many others? All these shopkeepers, those men in the square, who are they, and where did they come from? How deep do you want to dig, here? Because, yeah, I know things, but unfortunately, I can't talk about many of the things I know because to do so would be sedition, treason, even if this group is conducting criminal acts against the people of this country. I've probably said way too much. God damn, I hate this shit."

Duke leaned forward, crossing his arms on the metal table. "She's right, but I'm not bound to the same rules as my girl here," he said, his gaze lingering on her across the table. He had spoken so fondly of her.

"No, Duke, but you're not such a dumbass as to not know that you could be disappeared, dumped in some hole, never to be heard from again, and there would be jack shit I could do about it," she said. "You'd just be gone, and even I wouldn't have any idea where to look for what was left of you."

An odd smile pulled at Duke's lips. "You know, I worked on a story years back. Had a source who provided documents detailing how the CIA planned to drug criminals awaiting trial in a prison hospital ward in a bid to develop improved techniques in drug interrogation. Another detailed the CIA's interest in developing ways to cause amnesia in humans using experiments, no matter how weird, deadly, or dangerous. Convenient way to get someone to forget what you've done to them, what they've seen, or what they've been part of. If that's what's going on here, we're going to need more than a few curious souls. What's the plan? This isn't going to be a matter of walking in and walking out. We've got a heavily guarded lab and potentially a secret government, which just about reduces our odds to less than zero."

"Look." Chogan pointed discreetly across the street. The chief and the men were now walking away from the town hall in the square, each headed in a different direction.

"We need to find out who they are and what they're up

to tonight." Raul nodded at them. "After Lydia and the kids are safe, then we'll dig deeper. The only thing I'm interested in is getting them out and finding some measure of justice for Wyatt."

Just then, Jeffrey strode out of the coffeehouse and stopped behind him, leaning down and pressing the palms of his hands flat on the metal table between Raul and Duke. "Just got a little warning inside to be careful and stay out of town tonight."

"You mean because of the hunting party?" Raul said in a low voice.

Whereas Jeffrey frowned, Chogan remained stoic, giving nothing away. His dark eyes flickered between them. Then he sighed, lifting his hand. "I think we need to split up while it's daylight to find out who those men are and what this hunting party is about. Then we need to figure out a plan to get Raul's family out of here." Chogan let his gaze settle on him.

Robin, who had said nothing at all, now scraped back his chair, standing up. "Okay, Chogan, I'll tag along with you. Say we meet up back at the motel by three?"

"Jeffrey, you and Duke see what you can find out about those men who were with the chief in the square," Harley said from where she sat, then nodded at Raul. "That leaves you and me."

Out of anyone there, he wondered why he wasn't more uneasy with a spook wanting to tag along with him.

"So what are you planning?" Duke asked as he slipped on his sunglasses, stood, and pushed his empty mug to the middle of the table.

"I don't know," Harley said. "I think that depends on what you find out. From there, we figure out a way to get into the lab, rescue Lydia and the kids, and get back out without any of us getting killed. Because as I see it, there's no turning back now."

Raul watched as the others walked away, and Harley fell in beside him as he took in the empty square, surrounded by shops with flower boxes in front.

"What do you say, Raul? Shall we take a drive?" She tapped him on the arm.

"You know, Harley, I can't quite figure you out. The one thing I know about the CIA is you can't trust them."

He didn't know what to expect, but she didn't flinch. Instead, an odd smile touched her lips. "Fair enough," was all she said.

"So where, exactly, are we going on this drive?"

She tilted her head and glanced up at one of the streetlights surrounding the town square. "Someplace we're not being watched," she said.

Raul looked up at the lights and the buildings, knowing well that everywhere they went, a camera was on them. As they left the square, a chilling breeze swept through, carrying whispers that seemed to echo with the town's many secrets.

CHAPTER 12

The pickup truck's engine hummed a low, steady growl as Harley and Raul once again left the town limits behind. There was something unnerving about leaving a place where all eyes were on them.

"Are you sure about this?" Raul's fingers tightened around the steering wheel, his knuckles whitening.

"Positive," Harley said, her voice unwavering as she checked the rearview mirror for any signs of pursuit. "Just drive. Take the gravel trail here; it's a back way to that underground lab."

The side road was barely noticeable, and Raul hadn't even known it existed. It wound its way around, bringing them closer to the hidden door in the hillside. He turned off the truck, noting the trees in the distance and the absence of anything else around.

"Should I ask how you knew about this trail?"

Harley only shrugged and gestured toward the hillside. "From here, it kind of looks like the mouth of Hades, ready to swallow up everything around." She yanked the truck door open, stepped out, and closed it behind her, leaving Raul staring after her.

"Damn spooks," he muttered under his breath, feeling anything but comfortable. He couldn't help but wonder how he'd gone from being alone to now having five other people he knew little about in his life. Harley was already at the steel door and had picked the lock, and she gestured sharply with her chin for him to follow.

"Let's move," she whispered, stepping inside and holding the door until Raul reached it.

"Hey, you want to let me in on what the plan is?"

She hesitated a second in the doorway, looking down the well-lit corridor he'd been in less than twenty-four hours earlier. "Just seeing what's here, what we can find out, and confirming what I suspect is happening here."

He didn't know what to make of that. He stepped inside, and she let the door close quietly behind them. The secrecy of this place, and Harley, bothered him in ways he'd never experienced before. Maybe because he didn't know where her allegiance truly lay.

The corridor stretched before them, an artery of cold concrete. Harley led the way to an elevator and pulled a pair of black gloves from her pocket, then slipped them on before pressing the button. Then she held her finger to her lips, flicking her gaze up to a blinking red light above them. Raul found himself looking back to the exit, now a long way away, when the elevator doors opened.

"Harley, how do you know where we're going?" Raul asked, anxiety creeping into his voice, as he hesitated to step in after her.

"Research," she muttered, reaching for his arm and giving it a yank. He stepped in, and she stared at the digital panel on the wall as the doors closed. Their descent was a silent plunge into the bowels of the earth. Raul couldn't help but wonder if he was the one being led to slaughter.

"Get that worried look off your face," Harley said.

"You know what scares me? It seems you know your way around, and you're far too comfortable. So how much do you know about this place?"

The elevator slowed, and the digital display read sublevel three. Harley was staring right at him, her expression one of frustration. "You're skeptical, not trusting," she said. "Down here, these deep-state places are similar in more ways than not. Look like you belong and keep your head down. Don't talk."

That was all she said. As the door opened, Raul's chest tightened, unsure of what awaited them on the other side. They stepped out into a wide-open area that gleamed white, all steel and concrete, secure doors with locks and keypads. He thought he heard voices.

Harley found a door that wasn't locked, opened it a crack, and gestured for him to follow. "Come on," she hissed.

The room appeared to be a locker room filled with white lab overalls and coats. Harley didn't hesitate, pulling a set onto her slender frame, covering her street clothes entirely. She snapped the slipcovers over her shoes with practiced ease.

"Disguise is half the game," she said in response to Raul's worried expression. "Now look the part. Act like you belong."

Raul complied, his movements clumsy with tension, but he managed to fit into the sterile garb. "You never answered me," he said. "Should I be worried about how comfortable you seem down here?"

She was already around the corner, but she stepped back, her brows raised. "You should be worried about what they're doing to your family," she said. She had him there, and she started again toward the door, looking right and left before gesturing for him to follow.

They passed a woman dressed similarly, who walked past them without a glance. He wondered how many were working down there, part of whatever dark agenda was unfolding. Ahead was a wall of glass leading to a room with banks of computers and equipment.

Harley pushed open the glass door and peered inside. "No one here."

Raul watched the hallway. A man who had just exited the room was headed down the hall in the opposite direction. "What are you looking for?" he asked in a low voice, glancing over to see Harley tapping away at a computer keyboard.

"This," was all she said. He looked over her shoulder to see a map sprawled across the screen. "I knew it would be here, schematics of the lab and the trail of funding. Looks like it traces back to a private nonprofit agency— nothing more than a hydra of government tendrils and dark money, all funded by taxpayers, is my guess." Harley's eyes narrowed as she stared at the screen.

Raul quickly glanced down the hall. "Harley, you need to hurry. Being in the halls is one thing, but being caught in here is going to be a problem."

"Ah, here it is. Project titles: genetic manipulation, mind control, hunting games for the amusement of the invisible elite."

"Jesus," Raul breathed, looking down the hall and then back at her. "You got a way to copy that? Tick-tock, Harley."

He thought he heard her swear under her breath. She pulled out a small memory stick from inside her jacket and shoved it into the computer. "Just let me download, and then we're out of here."

Raul heard voices. Someone was approaching. "Ah, shit. You done? Someone's coming."

"Just another minute."

He didn't look back as he opened the door and stepped out, then walked right toward someone in the same white coveralls and bumped into him.

"So sorry, didn't see you there," Raul said.

The man, middle aged and slender, frowned at him. "Watch where you're going. You should know better down here," he said. "Hey, I don't recall seeing you around here before."

Harley had emerged from the room and was walking straight at them.

"Hey! What were you doing in there?" the man snapped.

Raul's heart skipped a beat as he tried to think of a response.

"My job, checking on the equipment," Harley said curtly, tapping Raul's arm. "You have that meeting with the director. You're going to be late."

It was the mention of the director that had the man hurrying the other way, he figured.

"Shit, that was too close for me. You get it?" Raul asked as they walked away.

Harley held up the stick. "With more than I expected, I'm sure. Let's move."

Raul was already turned around. Harley pulled him right down a corridor, and they found themselves in front of one-way glass, beyond which women in hospital gowns sat in chairs, vacant-eyed. His heart thudded, and his breath caught. Lydia was among them, slumped in a rocking chair. Raul reached out as if to touch the glass, but Harley pulled him back.

"Sweet Jesus, there's Lydia," he said.

"We can't help her now. We've got to go." Her grip was strong, but Raul yanked his arm away.

"We can't leave her. I'm *not* leaving her."

"You listen to me, Raul. We need to get out of here now. We know she's here, but we don't know the extent of what's happening. If we grab her, we blow any chance of finding your nieces and nephews. Think, Raul! We come back better prepared, after I have a chance to look at what I downloaded. Then we have a plan, and help. You know this. Come on, let's go."

Reluctantly, Raul followed Harley as she led the way back through the winding corridors. They passed a heavy steel door with a small window, through which children were hooked up to machines, their faces twisted in distress. Scientists or doctors moved around the room.

"We can't worry about that now," Harley said, urging Raul to keep moving.

"I have questions—"

"And now's not the time," she cut him off in a low voice.

Raul sighed, his thoughts on the children and his family as they made their way back outside.

Once at the truck, Raul leaned against the door, watching as Harley stashed their disguises behind a bush. "Meet at the motel at three. Robin, Chogan, Duke, and Jeffrey—they need to see this," she said, holding up the memory stick.

"Can't shake the feeling this is nothing new for you.

What we saw there, what are they doing?" Raul asked as he climbed in and started the truck.

"You think experimenting is anything new?" Harley had joined him in the truck and was staring ahead. "I guarantee you they convinced someone of the importance of their work, that sacrificing a few is worth it for the greater good, for the many. You know what? The average person could never wrap their head around the government disappearing people for places like this. There are signed agreements, classified. All of this is justified somewhere. I'm not shitting you."

Her simmering anger was evident as she continued. "What I saw while downloading is that there's an entire section of this agency devoted to monitoring the public. They stay ahead of anyone who discovers something they shouldn't. I won't say where, but they have entire agencies and divisions that study and keep track of everything posted on social media, building intelligence reports. They gauge reactions to events, foresee uprisings, decide which people could become a problem after realizing their government has lied to them. I think this place is a full-service site, and I suspect this so-called hunting party is likely a practice scenario. But for what objective?"

Raul turned the pickup truck around and drove back the way they'd come, leaving behind the oppressive darkness of the underground tunnels. But he couldn't shake the lingering sense of urgency and danger. He knew he couldn't turn back now, even if it meant facing the unknown horrors that awaited him above ground and below. What they'd discovered meant there was no one they could call for help, because whatever this was, it was way beyond the reach of the average cop, federal agent, or politician.

CHAPTER 13

Gravel crunched underfoot as Raul and Harley returned to the seedy motel that had become their impromptu command center. The late afternoon sky was a bruised canvas of purples and blues, and a wind came out of nowhere from the north as he followed Harley around back to where their motley crew of truth-seekers had gathered at two picnic tables in the far corner of the parking lot, flanked by the encroaching shadows of trees. The spot would have been perfect except for the rusty dumpster that flanked the other side.

"Anything?" Raul said in a low voice as he stopped at the end of the table, where Jeffrey sat across from Robin.

Duke, beside Jeffrey, was typing something into a laptop. "Ralph and Bully," he said, spitting out the names like they left a bad taste in his mouth. "The men in the square with the chief, and that's if those are even their real names. It's like they're ghosts. No paper trails, no digital footprints. Nothing."

Jeffrey Snider, with his farmer's tan and weathered hands, leaned forward, the table creaking under his weight. "The chief's dirty, for sure. But he's just the front man. Whoever's pulling the strings is higher up than we thought."

"Much higher," Duke echoed, shaking his head, eyes not leaving the screen.

"Chogan and I learned a bit about the hunting games." Robin seemed tense as he leaned forward, resting his crossed arms on the picnic table. He flicked his gaze up to Raul, his blue eyes determined. "A mechanic behind the town council let slip that some big names are coming into town tonight. Some sick version of hide and seek."

"Let me see that," Harley said abruptly, reaching for Duke's laptop as she sat on the other side of him. Her fingers were already poised with her USB stick.

"Now, what do you have there?" Duke asked. He had relinquished his laptop, letting Harley slide it in front of her and insert the stick into the port. Everyone was quiet. Chogan had walked around the table and stood behind Harley.

"Look at this," she said. "Experiments, schematics, an entire division for cyber warfare."

"Jesus," murmured Chogan, his stoic demeanor cracking ever so slightly as he peered over her shoulder. Raul found himself walking around to see what Duke had pointed at on the screen, pages of documents, maps, and outlines.

"How much information do you have there? And is it going to help us?" Raul asked. Harley made a face as she looked back at him. He wondered whether he was the only one who was feeling the urgency of the situation.

"I have no idea, but there's so much here, it would take me months to look through all of it," Harley said. "This is some weird shit out of MK Ultra, like a battle for the minds of man. It seems they've targeted their victims. Honestly, I've seen some really disturbing things, but this looks like upscale brain warfare, similar to what they did to the American POWs." Harley sighed and gave her head a shake.

Maybe it was the odd looks from Robin and Jeffrey that had Raul saying softly, "Not everyone has heard the stories, Harley."

She gave a nod and gestured to the group. "After Vietnam, there were stories of returning soldiers who had been prisoners of war parroting the communist propaganda they'd been hearing for weeks, months, years. It happened softly at first, not overtly, and then suddenly it was as though they had different personalities. But this, just scratching the surface, looks more centered around behavior modification. Here, it talks about experimenting via electroshock therapy, hypnosis, polygraphs, radiation, and a variety of drugs, toxins, chemicals, and more. The only thing I can tell you that I know of these programs is that they prey on the most vulnerable in society, from the mentally impaired to the emotionally traumatized, especially those who won't be missed or lack resources." Harley pulled up another document and opened another folder, and Duke swore under his breath at whatever he was reading.

"I don't understand what this place is for, this pristine town," Duke said. "The underground lab, how does this all tie together…?"

Chogan shut his eyes and gave his head a shake. "If you can control the minds of the people, you can control the world."

Harley looked back to Chogan and then over to Raul.

"It's going to take some time to figure out the map, where they're keeping everyone and why."

That was what bothered Raul about this, the slow slog. "I get it," he said. "I understand now how someone close to a situation feels, with loved ones involved. They never understand the planning, insisting we just go in and get it done." He let out a heavy sigh. No one said anything. "I think our first priority has to be tonight. We focus on the hunting game," he continued at last, feeling as if he were eating his own guts out. "Harley, you keep digging into this. We need a way in to find Lydia and those kids."

Harley was staring at the computer screen, gesturing to it. "Well, this is a map of the town, and I think the main entrance to the lab is here, which is in the town hall. I wonder if this is where everyone comes and goes. Would think the security here would be tight."

"Maybe we stick with the entrance in the woods," Jeffrey said with confidence. "Didn't you slip in and out? That's what we did last night, unnoticed."

"I guarantee you we were not unnoticed, which bothers me in ways I can't quite put my finger on," Harley said, then let her gaze linger on Raul before she continued. "With this level of sophistication, I'm feeling out of my depth here, guys. Have I said that yet? Maybe I should. What I'm seeing here scares the ever-living shit out of me, and I don't scare easily." Harley fisted her hands.

Quiet had only just settled around them when Raul heard the distant chopping of a helicopter, not just one but two flying overhead, large and black, the sound of the blades almost deafening.

"Anyone else questioning what those black choppers mean?" he vaguely heard Jeffrey say.

"Nothing good," Duke said. "My guess is they're

connected to this hunting party, maybe guests of honor or something."

As they passed overhead, heading toward the town, the vibration rumbled in the ground beneath his feet. It only added to the unease that had continued to build.

"Or another black project, something off the books," Harley cut in. "Let's keep our heads down and eyes open."

"Or maybe they're onto us and our poking around," Chogan said. "I'm convinced it was too easy to get into their underground lab without being caught."

Everyone looked his way. He had only voiced the exact thing that had been bothering Raul.

Harley had been quietly studying another map. She glanced back up at Chogan. "It may be all of the above or something else. Whatever's going on here, no one is going to want us talking about it. I guarantee you someone knew we were in there. Maybe they haven't figured out who we are, or maybe they know everything we're doing and they're fucking with us, basically walking us right into a trap." She shrugged.

Jeffrey and Robin stilled as the fear of what she'd said sank in. Robin looked over his shoulder and then back at them, and he had lifted his hand as if to say something when Harley cut in again.

"Here," she said, pointing to a cluster of buildings near the town square. "There's an underground tunnel system that connects several buildings in this area."

"That could be useful." Duke leaned in, staring at the laptop.

Raul wasn't as sure. "Sounds like a lot of exits, a lot of eyes, and more ways we could be caught," he said. "There's so much going on here. The only feeling I'm getting is that I'll never have justice for Wyatt, and Lydia and the kids could be lost. After all, we have no fucking idea what they've done to her, to them, and where the kids are—if they're even here."

No one said anything. He had expected at least one to say this was too much for them and they were out of there. Chogan's hand landed on his shoulder.

"Raul, I get it," Harley said, closing the laptop, "but letting your head go to the worst case isn't going to help. Stay focused. I'll find where they're keeping Lydia and figure out the best way to get them out. I can do that much. The rest of you, right now, the priority has to be this hunting game."

She had really sounded like a boss. Raul realized she knew things in this spook game that he might not want to know.

HOURS LATER, AS THE SUN WENT DOWN, RAUL STOOD AT THE edge of the town square, watching Chogan approach from around the corner, glancing back once over his shoulder.

"You get the feeling something is off?" was all Chogan said as he reached him, hands fisted at his sides, before pulling his cell phone from the pocket of his jean jacket.

"In my bones. Too quiet. It's almost as if we're on a movie set and everyone has packed up and gone home for the day." He knew it was an odd comment. He spotted Jeffrey walking their way, wearing a black hoodie, and Robin and Duke cutting across the square from the other side. "Well, this doesn't look good," he added, feeling the oppressive silence.

"Damn it," Jeffrey cursed under his breath as he got closer. "I had the feeling it was too easy. The intel on the hunting game, did we get it wrong? Maybe it's not what we think."

"Diversion, is my guess," Chogan stated flatly, his dark eyes scanning the area with vigilance. "Look here, not there. Yeah, they know why we're here and what we're doing. They're probably watching us right now, keeping score, showing us they're still one step ahead of us and hold all the cards."

Robin was now running toward them, Duke trying to keep up. "Look over there," he called out, pointing toward the town hall. "Behind is a garage. Duke said a steady stream of cars are coming out."

Duke was out of breath as he reached them. "There's a tunnel underground," he said. "I swear, the door opened to reveal an underground garage or something, and the steel floor lifted, and cars, pickups, too many vehicles to count drove out, one after the other."

Raul heard the cars. "There are more coming this way," he said, just as a minivan, a white pickup, and a car emerged, driving out the way they had come into town, leading toward the motel. He stared, trying to see the faces of the drivers, blinking because he couldn't be sure.

"Lydia," he whispered as an older four-door sedan rolled past them, just within range of the streetlight's early evening glow. In the driver's seat was a woman who looked just like Lydia, staring straight ahead. She never looked his way. It was just a second, but deep in his gut, he knew it was her. As he took a step around Robin, following the taillights of the last vehicle, he had the sinking feeling he was too late.

"Did you say Lydia?" A hand rested on his shoulder.

His heart was hammering against his ribs, and sweat beaded on his forehead even though the evening air was cool. "Behind the wheel of that rusty sedan. Not her car, but yeah, I know that was her. It was only a flash, a second, but long enough." He stared down the vacant stretch of asphalt leading away from the automotive shop. The convoy of vehicles had vanished into the night, leaving only the echo of engines and a town that was eerily quiet.

"Where are they going?" Raul muttered, his voice barely cutting through the thickening tension. No one said anything, but he hadn't expected that anyone would.

"Two different directions, my guess. Maybe we have it wrong on what this hunting game is," Chogan replied. His usually stoic face creased with concern when he heard the squealing of tires and looked over to see an older Jeep screeching to a stop.

"Guys, hey!" Harley yelled from across the square, where she jumped out of a Jeep YJ that had seen better days. She was already running their way in a gray pullover and blue jeans, pounding the pavement and gesturing. "We have it wrong," she said as she reached them. "They've been planning and practicing here for a staged attack. I don't have any idea of the what and why, but I found the where, in West Virginia, at one of the largest shopping malls there. The vehicles I passed…" Harley gestured behind her. "Look, I was going through all the files, and there was a plan. They're actors, and they've been practicing. There was video footage, filmed right here. And something else…" Harley had stopped, and Raul suspected he wasn't going to like what he was about to hear. She looked his way as she continued. "These people, they've been programmed in a way. It's like their minds have been hijacked to perform whatever sick scenario's been planted there."

"Mind control? Sorry, don't know if I buy that," Jeffrey said. "It's too out there in science fiction land for me."

Raul wanted to tell him to stop talking. He didn't want to take the time to explain to him how things like that had been under way for a long time; he just hadn't expected to come face to face with it.

"Practicing for what, exactly?" Duke said. "Is that why all the vehicles have been driving out of here like a convoy? They have their plan, their orders, and now what?" He stopped, distracted. Someone was headed their way, and it took Raul a moment to realize it was Chief Walker.

He tapped Chogan on the shoulder. "We've got company," he murmured.

Everyone was now looking at the chief, who didn't appear out for a casual walk. He stopped right in front of them and hesitated, letting his gaze linger before it settled on Raul.

"You were warned to leave town," he said. "You've got no business here. You've been nosing around, poking your head into things that will get you removed permanently from the area. Listen up, because who you are is no secret: a military vet and town deputy, a journalist, a doctor, and a three-letter agency spook who's lost the plot. I can't quite figure out what a farmer and an Indian are doing with you all, though. Sorry to Injun boy for not being politically correct." He stepped closer to Chogan and jabbed a finger to his chest.

Raul sensed this could explode, and he slapped his hand over Chogan's chest to hold him back as he moved to step forward. "No," he said, shaking his head, feeling Chogan's anger, knowing the chief was trying to provoke. For some reason, he was zeroing in on Chogan.

The chief looked up and over Raul's head, and the way he did it had Raul glancing back and up to an old town clock.

"You've been doing your homework, Chief," Harley said, pulling her arms over her chest. "Here's ours. Tell us about the underground lab here and the buildings along Main Street that seem to have direct access. What is this a front for? All the cars just drove out of here, and now it seems unusually quiet, like everyone just up and left. What are you protecting?"

The chief said nothing, but the laugh under his breath seemed odd. His eyes flicked up again, past Raul, and he realized something was off.

"I remember a time I was undercover, running an op down in South America," Raul said. "It was in a little town that reminded me of old Germany, and there were these clocks around town that were used to watch and monitor people. The technology was off the charts. It could detect in seconds who you were, tracked everything from your bank, to your tax records, to your social media, everything you did online, everything you owned and bought, who you talked to, and if you said and did things that could be a problem for the powers that be. It was impressive, in a totalitarian kind of way, to monitor and make sure no one stepped out of line." Raul didn't know what kind of reply he expected from the chief.

"Effective, isn't it?" the chief said. "When you know it's right there, it scares you just enough, knowing everything you do and say has someone watching. Leaves you with a warm and tingly feeling and keeps you right where they want you, with that invisible leash on."

"What are you talking about?" Leave it to Jeffrey to openly question what the chief didn't seem to want to say.

Raul dragged his gaze over to him and then back to the chief.

"Just a walk down memory lane," Raul said. "I've seen a lot of places, corners of the world the average person will never see, kind of like that mass exodus of vehicles we just witnessed from underground."

The chief was nodding, taking them all in again. "Remember the rules here," he said. "No one out past nine. The clock is behind you, so keep an eye on it. You must be familiar with that little place in Guyana—what was it called, Jonestown? Makes you wonder why it is that some people are unable to think for themselves and are led around so easily."

"That sounds a lot like brainwashing," Harley interrupted, causing the chief to finally look at her.

"Don't forget," he said. "You're running out of time." Then he turned his gaze back to Raul for a moment before walking away in the direction he had come from.

"What was that all about?" Robin asked.

"I was expecting some kind of intimidation or aggression to force us out, but it was surprisingly cordial," Duke remarked. Raul, however, was more focused on the chief's departure. Everything about their interaction had seemed backward compared to his previous perceptions of the chief.

"We may have it all wrong," Raul said in a low voice. Harley followed his gaze to where the chief walked across the square and then across the road. Chogan, too, hadn't pulled his gaze from where the chief had gone.

"I don't get it," Jeffrey said.

Raul glanced back and up to the clock. "So they know everything about us, who we are, where we're from, and yet we're still here, walking around. Seems like they're one step ahead of us because they know what we're doing next. It's too quiet here. Lydia drove out of here, but who's left?"

No one said anything. Each of them had glanced past him, looking up at the clock.

"Maybe we shouldn't talk here," Jeffrey finally said.

Harley shook her head and started walking, then stopped for a second, looking at Raul and then Duke. "It's a nice night for a walk," she said.

Chogan leaned in closer as they all fell in and headed across the square where the chief had gone. "Let's go have a word with the mechanic," he said. "I have this feeling he knows more, and then I think we should consider splitting up. You know, cover our bases, go after the ones who left, and the rest stay here."

Raul watched as the others walked ahead, considering what Chogan was saying. "Because we don't know what's going on," he said, though he figured Chogan somehow understood this place on a level no one else did. "You think the kids are still here?"

"Maybe," Chogan said. "But one thing's for sure: We need to act fast, before it's too late."

CHAPTER 14

The hushed crunch of gravel underfoot was the only sound as the six approached the abandoned garage. Cold air whispered through the desolate space, and Raul's breath misted before him. He clenched his jaw tightly, determination driving him. The ramp to the underground was shut, and if he hadn't known the metal floor was hiding the entrance, he realized he wouldn't have seen it. Chogan, a large man who moved with surprising quietness, led the way to the back, where a feeble light flickered.

"There's no one here," Jeffrey murmured from behind him as they stepped into a cluttered, grimy office featuring a metal desk and an old metal filing cabinet. Then, they noticed someone.

"Out!" Chogan reached down, grabbing the man in blue coveralls from his makeshift hideaway in the corner.

"Talk," Duke said, getting right in his face. "The cars, West Virginia—why? We know you all lied. The hunting games and the big names coming in were just diversions. Who told you to lie to us?"

Raul pulled his hand over the back of his neck in frustration, feeling everything spiraling out of control.

"Let him go," came a voice from behind them. It was the chief, striding into the dimly lit shop. Raul had never heard him coming.

The mechanic, with short dark hair and a neatly trimmed beard, stepped away, darting his gaze to the chief, the only person he seemed to fear.

"Norm, head on out," the chief said, nodding slightly. "I've got this."

"Sure thing, Chief," the mechanic replied. He glanced at Raul for only a second before walking past him and then Harley, who stood, arms crossed, behind the chief, and out the door.

The chief said nothing as he walked over to the wall at the back of the shop and pressed a large yellow button. The hydraulic groan filled the space as the steel floor lifted, revealing the ramp to the hidden underground garage.

"Remember Congressman Rollins from West Virginia?" the Chief began, his voice cutting through the clamor of hydraulics. "The one who's been opposed to the new federal budget, holding things up because buried deep in there seems to be free housing, monthly food stipends, and subsidies for immigrants, along with various other perks? How often do you have a congressman who actually reads what's hidden in those budgets? Heard he was planning on showing up at a big shopping mall opening for his state."

Raul had picked up the crumbs being dropped.

"This Rollins fellow," the chief continued, "working in the country's best interest, trying to out the travesty that the citizens would be footing the bill. This country should be looking after the people here first, not giving it away, bringing in more illegals, more immigrants, while families here continue to struggle. Can you imagine?" he mused cynically. "Seems almost traitorous to some."

"So, they're going to kill him? Is that what this is about? Why all the cars?" Harley stepped closer, staring at the chief as the hydraulics slowly lifted the floor, now nearly drowning out their voices.

The chief sighed heavily. "You know how it works. One bullet...or maybe more. Create a diversion, and add in some crisis actors for when the shooting starts. The cameras of the news media will already be there because it's their congressman. Create panic, screams, running. Maybe some fake casualties for the cameras to blast all over the world. Maybe get that gun reform finally passed. Kill two birds with one stone."

The hydraulics quieted. The entire floor had lifted, at last revealing the ramp. The chief wiped his hands as he headed over to Raul and said cryptically, his voice low, "Level eight is where the kids are. Exit in the town square."

Raul's palms sweated. The uneasiness that continued to plague him had changed now to more of an urgency. "Fuck, I think it's time to split up," he said. "Harley, you, Robin, and Jeffrey need to get to that mall. Get a call in to the congressman." He glanced down into the underground garage as he looked over to Duke and Chogan. "You ready for this?" he said, wondering how anyone could be.

"Watch your back," was all Harley said before leading the way out of the shop, with Robin and Jeffrey hurrying after her.

"Jesus, you know I'm not a religious man," Duke remarked, beads of sweat visible on his brow, "but I've prayed more since arriving here in this madness than I've done in my life."

"Yeah, well, maybe that's not such a bad idea." Raul hesitated only another second before following Chogan down the ramp into the underground, the darkness swallowing them whole. The unease was palpable, but Raul couldn't shake the feeling that the chief's sudden willingness to assist could also be a trap, especially considering the unresolved situation with Wyatt's death. The one question he couldn't shake, what exactly was the chief's role in his friend's death?

Lights suddenly popped on above them. The underground garage was filled with luxury vehicles and a blacked-out bus. At the end, surrounded by concrete, was an elevator. Chogan pressed the button, and the steel doors opened. They stepped inside, and Raul tapped the digital screen, selecting level eight. His heart raced as the doors closed, and the elevator began to move.

"So, what's the plan?" Duke leaned in, his voice tense. Chogan looked on, shaking his head.

"Not a clue," Raul said. "I'm way out of my depth here. Eyes open, find the kids, and let's not get killed."

The elevator had come to a halt at level eight. They stepped out into a sterile corridor filled with the soft echoes of children. Raul moved cautiously along the wall until he stood before a solid glass window. The children stood behind it, all with shaved heads. The ones with their backs to them had black barcodes at the base of their necks.

"Holy shit, do you see that?" Duke's voice sounded odd and fairly distant, maybe because Raul couldn't shake the horror of what he was seeing. "Like cattle, catalog inventory. Are they stealing the identities of these kids? This is evil."

Raul turned to Chogan. "We need to get in there. Any idea how we get this open? Do you see how many children are in there?"

Chogan narrowed his gaze as if having a hard time seeing what they were seeing. He said nothing, then started walking, likely looking for a way in.

"Do you see your brother's kids?" Duke had already stridden past him, but Raul couldn't pull his gaze away from the kids. How many were there in that room? It seemed like he was in an observatory. He wondered whether they could see him, too, but he realized it was one-way glass. He didn't recognize the kids, but then, only a few were looking his way.

He heard the click and slide of the door with a hiss.

"Found it," was all Chogan said.

Raul was the first through the door. He took in all the kids as they turned to him, but it was the little girl, her blond hair just growing back, whose eyes, filled with fear, reminded him of his brother. He leaned down. "Hey, Pearlie, it's me, Uncle Raul. Your dad sent me to get you." His heart was hammering, and the ache that ripped through his heart nearly brought him to his knees. He did kneel, then, in front of his two-year-old niece, who was wearing the same white hospital gown all the kids were; they were all barefoot. He had to remind himself getting them out was the first priority. There would be time after to sort out what had happened to them there.

Pearlie had her arms around him, and he lifted her. Just then, another little hand touched him.

"Uncle Raul!" It was Clementine, his four-year-old niece, her voice so damn innocent. Then there was Arlis, seven, running over and throwing his arms around him. He was crying, and damn, Raul wanted to cry, too. He vaguely heard Duke and Chogan saying something to the other kids. He could feel their fear, and the smell that hit him was so sterile. Antiseptic, he figured, and that left him uneasy.

"Hey, hey, I got you," he said. "We're getting out of here. Do you know where Ruby and Samson are?"

The two girls said nothing, but Arlis gripped his coat and said, "They're not here. They're with the older kids."

Clementine was now whimpering, and he bent down to lift her in his other arm and said, "Listen, I'm getting you out of here, but I need you to be brave for me." He had said it more to Arlis, as Pearlie and Clementine had buried their faces against him.

He looked for Duke, who was in the hallway but hurried back into the room and gestured to him, his expression urgent and uneasy. "We've got to go," he said. "Come on. Let's get the kids out of here. Reunion time is later."

Chogan was on the other side of the room, having somehow managed to usher out the other kids. Duke was already at the elevator. They had seen no one, which surprised Raul.

"Arlis, come on," he said. "I'm getting you out of here. I know you've been through a lot, but I need you all to be quiet."

His nephew said nothing as he looked down, feeling his fear. He didn't let go of Raul's jacket.

"You can do this, boy," Raul said. "You just hang on to me."

Duke hurried over to him, taking in Arlis and the two girls. "Are they all here?"

Raul shook his head. "Just three. Arlis said the other two are with the older kids. Ruby is thirteen, Samson ten. We need to find them."

Duke had an odd look on his face. "Arlis, do you know where the older kids are?" he said.

The little boy was holding on to Raul's jeans with his tiny hand. He lifted his other hand and pointed just past where Chogan was at the elevator, ushering all the kids in. It was noisier than Raul had hoped.

"I'll check," was all Duke said before heading where Arlis had pointed down the hall, the other way. By the way Duke stopped and looked, Raul figured it was another window. He shook his head. "Empty. No one's here."

Chogan had his hand on the door of the elevator. "No time to wait," he said in a low voice. "Come on. We need to go before someone comes looking. If we have to come back, we will."

Raul moved, hurrying over to him with the kids in his arms. "Take my brother's kids. I'll stay and keep looking," he said, but Pearlie started crying, and then so did Clementine, both holding on to him with a death grip. "Ease up, girls. You're going to choke me."

"No, don't leave us!" Arlis cried, panicked. "Please, Uncle Raul!"

Duke touched his back, shaking his head. "No, we need to go," he said. "They're not here. Let's get these kids out, and then we'll come back."

Raul knew Duke was right, but it killed him to step into that elevator. Chogan had lifted a little boy in his arms, and they were all crammed in.

"It's okay. It's going to be okay," he said to his two nieces, who were trembling, gripping his jacket. Arlis stared up at him with hazel brown eyes that reminded him of Lydia. He wanted to say again that it was going to be okay, but he was filled with both relief and terror. They were still in this pit of hell. As he held the kids, his throat thickened with anger that had him wanting to weep. Who were the monsters who had put their hands on his brother's kids? He wanted to hunt every one of them down and permanently see to it that they were six feet under.

A hand touched his shoulder and squeezed, and he found himself looking over to Chogan. "Don't get stuck in your head. Shake it off," he said. "There will be time later to deal with the damage and what's happened. But now isn't the time."

As the elevator climbed back up, he knew Chogan was right, because he still needed to find Ruby and Samson, and then there was Lydia. It seemed a lifetime since he had driven into this nightmare, all because his good friend Wyatt had discovered something he wasn't supposed to see.

CHAPTER 15

"Are you sure it's in Huntington?" Robin said from the passenger side of Harley's old Jeep. Jeffrey was in the darkened back seat, on his phone, and her eyes flicked up to meet his in the rear-view mirror as she drove in the dead of night. She knew he was talking to Chogan. They had found the kids right where the chief had said they would be. Her heartbeat had kicked up, her hands damp on the wheel. She gave it a little more gas, already driving twenty over.

"The congressman is doing a meet and greet with his constituents after being at the mall opening for the kids just before noon." She'd put a call in to the congressman's office, but after hours meant voicemail, and she knew it was still too early for anyone to pick up.

"What is our plan, Harley? Are we just going to burst in and hope for the best? Why don't we just call the police? I still don't get it," Robin said. He was making valid points. Jeffrey, meanwhile, had hung up his phone.

Harley tightened her grip on the steering wheel. "What are we supposed to tell them, Robin?" she snapped, frustration evident in her voice. "That we stumbled upon a town that doesn't exist and a secret underground lab conducting experiments on people? And maybe that there's a convoy of vehicles heading to the new mall where the congressman will be present for an opening ceremony, but we're not sure what they're planning? The police won't take us seriously. They'll flag my number, or whoever calls, take our names, and before we know it, we'll be labeled as threats, possible terrorists, and thrown into some unknown location without any legal rights or representation, and no one will know where we are. Do you still want me to call?"

There was a brief moment of silence before Robin spoke up again. "Okay, fair enough. So what's our plan when we get to the mall? All I know is Lydia's face from the quick glimpse I got of her. I doubt I'll be able to spot her in a crowd."

Harley tapped her fingers against the steering wheel as she thought about their next move. "Well, while we figure that out, let's focus on the good news. Chogan said they found a group of kids, among them the three youngest of Raul's brother's. They're still looking for the older ones. So what do we do now?" The weight of responsibility had settled heavily on her shoulders. She couldn't help but wonder why everyone seemed to look to her for answers. "We find the congressman and scope out the area, looking for anything suspicious. If my guess is right, something is going down involving him. Our plan is simple: Find Lydia and hope she's coherent enough and willing to talk to us. That would be ideal. Otherwise, we'll have to improvise."

She glanced at Robin in the dimly lit Jeep, sensing his frustration and unease. As they passed a sign for Huntington, the city lights shimmered in the distance.

They were getting close now. Suddenly, Jeffrey's hand landed on her shoulder from the back seat.

"Just so you know, I have no idea what we're walking into or how to handle it, but I've got your back," he reassured her before pulling his hand away.

Robin shifted in his seat and let out a sigh. "It goes without saying that I expect we all have each other's backs, but I still want some kind of plan. I can handle unexpected injuries or emergencies, but guns and danger? That's way out of my comfort zone."

She reached over and patted his leg. "I'm right there with you, Robin. But the plan, unfortunately, is that I have no fucking idea."

AMID THE GRAND OPENING SIGNS AND CHILDREN'S foundation charity billboards, Harley stood at the back wall of the crowded area. A paper cup of takeout coffee appeared in front of her, handed to her by Robin, who stood beside her with his own cup. "Thanks," she said before taking a sip of the lukewarm and weak coffee. "Where's Jeffrey?"

"Searching for Lydia in the crowd," Robin replied, then took a drink from his cup, as well. "So we can't call the police, but do you have a contact in the CIA or someone we can warn? I'm feeling way out of my element here."

Harley dumped the rest of her coffee in a nearby trash can as she let out a sigh, dragging her gaze over the milling crowd. "I've been thinking a lot here, and the problem we're facing is that they're likely planning a diversion, some chaos. They want people to look there, not here. They have many ways to take the congressman out. It could be a sharpshooter or a heart-attack gun, depending on what the end goal is. The first would get a public outcry for gun reform. See all the cameras here? Everyone has their phones, too. The other is to not go for gun reform. The congressman dies of natural causes, or so they say, and is quietly replaced with their pick, and the problems he caused go away." She frowned, scanning the crowd, trying to get a feel for the stakes, but she felt so damn out of the loop.

"So, hypothetically, from your experience in your three-letter agency, what's the usual play here?"

She felt as if he were poking at her, trying to tie her to this in some way. "First, this isn't what I did in the agency," she said. "And, again, there are aspects of the agency and what goes on there that I can't and won't talk about because doing so will get me killed. Second, I have no fucking idea what's at play."

Just then, she spotted Jeffrey waving and making his way through the crowd toward them.

"What the hell is he doing?" Robin hissed as they watched him approach.

Jeffrey motioned with a sharp wave of his hand for them to follow, then looked back and gestured to the opposite side of the area, where a group of people were milling around. At the same time, a voice came over the loudspeaker, accompanied by clapping from the audience. Her heart raced as she hurried to catch up to Jeffrey, making her way through the crowd, Robin close behind her.

"I found Lydia," Jeffrey said as they maneuvered through the crowd, who were facing the stage and clapping. "She's wearing a volunteer badge. Come on."

"Excuse me, sorry about that," she muttered to those

they passed as they followed Jeffrey to the other side of the area. There was a woman with light shoulder-length hair, wearing a brown ballcap and red coveralls pinned with a volunteer badge. She had a bright smile, and for a moment, Harley wasn't sure this was Lydia, but Jeffrey was already in front of her again.

"Lydia," he began, "this is Harley and Robin. We're friends of Raul Booth, your brother-in-law."

She made a face and stepped back. "Are you talking to me? I think you have me confused with someone..." She waved them away almost dismissively.

Harley reached for Jeffrey's shoulder. "Hey, you may have the wrong person," she whispered, but he was adamant, and the expression he tossed her way was pure annoyance.

"No, I do not. Faces I'm good at," he snapped, then turned back to the woman and continued. "Lydia, Raul found your three youngest kids, Pearlie, Arlis, and Clementine."

She appeared confused, her brow furrowed. "What?" She took a step back again, her pupils large in her brown eyes, unusually so, as if she was on something.

"Jeffrey, did Raul send you a photo of the other kids, the older two?" Robin asked, but Harley didn't look away from the woman. Maybe Jeffrey was right; something in her expression seemed so lost.

"Yeah, right here." Jeffrey pulled out his phone, and Harley leaned in as he opened the photo Raul had texted him, showing Lydia, holding a baby, with four kids and a bearded man beside her with an arm around her, who she realized had to be Raul's brother. He held out his phone to Lydia.

"This is you right here, Lydia, with your children and your husband," Jeffrey said.

Harley looked behind Lydia, over to a group of kids by the entrance, but not before seeing the utter shock and horror in Lydia's brown eyes. She stilled and lifted her hand, touching the phone.

"Hey, Robin, take a look," Harley said, pointing behind him. "Are those the older two there? It looks like them."

Before he could turn to look, a boom shook the floor and walls, followed by screams and shouts. Her first instinct was to duck. Car alarms shrieked outside, and Jeffrey was now holding on to Lydia. Robin was already running past her, and someone yelled, "Get down!"

The unmistakable grind of metal on metal went right through her. Just in time, they all ducked as the metal scaffolding above the stage came crashing down. Through the chaos and dust, Harley realized Robin and the kids were nowhere in sight.

CHAPTER 16

As the beat-up pickup truck jolted along the rough road, which had one too many potholes, Raul couldn't shake the feeling that something sinister was following them. He stole a glance beside him, where the three youngest children huddled together on the bench seat, fast asleep, though their sleep was anything but peaceful. His grip on the steering wheel tightened as his heart raced. Just then, his cell phone rang, startling him. He quickly answered it while keeping an eye on little Clementine, who was snuggled up against him in the passenger seat, breathing shakily. An unknown number had appeared on the screen.

He answered hesitantly with a simple, "Hello?"

"It's Harley. We found them."

Emotion came out of nowhere, making him want to weep. He glanced again at his brother's kids, his nieces and nephew, who were his primary and only concern right now. Arlis was fast asleep, leaning against the passenger door, wearing Raul's coat, which was way too big on him. The girls were wrapped in an old orange and red Native

American blanket he kept in the back of his pickup. Duke and Chogan had taken the other children to Abingdon, to the sheriff's office, hoping to find their parents in the system. But these three, these were his business now. His brother's kids, his nieces and nephews, were his responsibility.

"You found Lydia and the kids, Ruby and Samson?" he said, his voice rough. "Are they okay?"

He should pull over, but the feeling that they weren't safe still lingered. Maybe that was why he couldn't fight the urge to check the rear-view mirror over and over.

"Lydia and the kids are alive," Harley said, "but she's out of it, Raul. Rambling about things that make no sense. Duke called and let me know he and Chogan have managed to get the other kids to Abingdon. Last he said, they were on their way to the county hospital even though he warned the sheriff of the danger of that. I wonder if the sheriff believes him. What we saw is almost unbelievable. How do you put it into words without sounding batshit crazy? Shit's going to fly, Raul. I can just feel it. But I have to tell you, and I think you already know this, whatever deep-state agency had those kids, no sheriff is going to be able to stop them from retrieving what they believe are their assets. Chogan said he won't leave because of that."

Raul gave his truck a little more gas, feeling the sidearm that was always with him tucked into the back of his faded jeans. That deep dread wouldn't leave him. He had never feared a shootout, but it was a different ball game, here and now, with the three little ones. "You think those kids we found will just disappear before they have a chance to find where they came from and who their parents are?" he said. He thought he already knew the answer, but Harley likely knew more from the spook agency she had worked for.

She let out a heavy sigh. "I think the minute an administrative clerk at that small county hospital starts typing any mention of those kids into the computer, it will be flagged in seconds, and any number of agencies or agents will descend on the place. Could be a social worker or a federal agent, but whoever it is will have the authority to grab them, with or without a stop to the hospital administrator. The secret warrant will be signed by a federal judge, citing national security, with details redacted. The hospital staff will probably be ordered not to talk about it, maybe forced to sign NDAs. It will be like those kids were never there. Maybe, by some miracle, the sheriff will manage to work faster and find the parents. Unfortunately, hope is all I have."

Exactly what Raul didn't want to hear. He already knew he was playing with fire.

"I need to take my brother's kids to the hospital," he said. "I don't know what those motherfuckers did. Are you telling me someone will show up for them or be waiting there?"

"I don't know for sure, Raul. Maybe they've figured out messing with you would be dangerous. But you'll never win against the military-industrial complex. It's too big, too dangerous, and has tentacles in every system, reaching further than you can imagine. Take them home to Asher first. I'm bringing Lydia and her kids to you."

He nodded, more to himself than anything. "They marked them like cattle, shaved heads and barcodes. I've never seen this before."

"Chogan told me," Harley said. "Look, Raul, this may sound cold, but I'm going to say it anyway: Whatever physical markings you see on those kids are nothing compared to what they've done. That's only surface stuff. Everything you don't see is likely much worse."

He really didn't want the kids hearing him talk, knowing there was so much ugliness in this world. He had reached the turn that would lead to his brother's place, and he took it. "All right, I'll go to Asher's first, but I already know my brother isn't going to sit back and hide. He'll want them checked over. Damn, this is going to gut him… I haven't figured out how to tell him."

There was silence for a moment.

"My advice, Raul? Don't overthink it. We'll be there soon," was all she said before hanging up.

At last, he rounded the bend where thick trees opened up to reveal his brother's place. He spotted his dog first, as the screen door had swung open before he even killed the engine. His brother was wearing the same overalls he'd been wearing when he left. Dawg was woofing and running his way. Asher seemed happy, smiling, as he lifted his hand in a wave and stepped down off the wooden porch, bearded and disheveled.

Raul turned off the truck and opened the door, the kids stirring. "Stay here," was all he said as he stepped out and closed it, wondering whether maybe he should have called and warned his brother.

"Hey, you're a sight for sore eyes. How did it go? I can tell you I didn't sleep well, worrying about you." His brother stopped, maybe at the look on his face, which he couldn't hide. "How bad? What did you find out about Wyatt?"

Raul took a step toward him and then another, shaking his head, remembering what Harley had said—don't overthink it. "Asher, I found your kids," he said. "They were in that town, and Lydia too. I have Clementine, Pearlie, and Arlis in the truck."

Asher had already stormed past him, and Raul recognized the moment his overprotective father instinct kicked in.

"Before you open that door, Asher, prepare yourself. Something was done to them. Their heads are shaved, and they have barcodes tattooed on them. There were other kids there. Whatever experiments they were doing..." He reached for Asher's arm, seeing horror staring back at him. "That's all I know, Asher. I drove right here. Friends of mine have Lydia, Ruby, and Samson."

His brother yanked open the truck door. "Hey, Pearlie, come here," he murmured. "Arlis, Clementine..." Emotion had roughened his voice. He reached for the girls as Arlis climbed down. "Who did this to my kids, Raul?"

Dawg was right there beside him, wanting attention, his tail wagging. He reached down and rubbed him, then gave him a hug before looking back over to Asher, with all three kids in his arms. Arlis was crying, and so was Clementine now, but two-year-old Pearlie just leaned her head on Asher's shoulder, burying her face in his neck.

He knew his brother was going to be hard to handle, and it would be harder for him to wrap his head around what Raul already suspected had been done to the kids. "I don't know everything, Asher, of what happened to them, but they were in that town where Wyatt went. All the craziness Wyatt was talking about when he phoned..." He stopped and let his gaze linger on the children, not wanting to get into the horror of what he suspected they'd endured.

"Hey, are you hungry?" Asher asked the kids. He wouldn't look at Raul; he was already carrying them to the house.

Even though Dawg had followed right behind Asher, Raul found it easier to stay where he was, watching the smoke from the chimney. He knew his brother would only demand answers, the kind Raul didn't have, just uncomfortable theories he'd pieced together. He knew, too, that there was more, much more.

He lingered outside the screen door, hearing the scrape of a chair inside. The kids were saying something. His dog gave him a wag of his tail as he lay down on the wooden porch.

"Good boy, I missed you," Raul said, running his hand over the dog's head. Then he pulled open the screen door. The welcoming squeak had his brother looking over to him. He stood at the table with a knife, a jar of peanut butter, and a loaf of bread. The kids were sitting on the bench, unusually stoic, as Asher made a sandwich for each of them. For a moment, the back and forth sounded almost normal, but he knew the kids were far from the joyful innocents they'd once been.

"There you go," Asher said. "I don't have any milk, but I'll pick some up." He went to the sink to fill glasses with water, and it was only then that Raul noticed the slight tremble in his brother's hands. As he set the small cups in front of the kids, Asher looked up at him with an ache in his eyes. "You just sit there and eat," he said. "I want to talk to your uncle a minute."

Raul didn't move, watching his brother look over his kids again before fisting his hands. Asher was twisted up in knots, and he still had no idea of what Raul had seen, what he'd pulled his children from.

"Raul, my kids—look at them," he said quietly, his voice shaking with barely contained rage. "What happened? What sick motherfucker did this? I need a doctor to look at them. They're not okay; anyone can see that. They're terrified."

"I'm not sure going to a hospital right now is a wise choice," Raul said. "Think about it, Asher. Where I found them and Lydia, what I saw there was beyond anything I've seen. These people will be watching all the hospitals. The reach they have is beyond what I can comprehend. They'll come for the kids…"

Fire flashed in Asher's eyes as he leaned in toward him. He had never been quick to anger, but by God, when he got there, there was no reasoning with him. "A wise choice," he said. "Those are hospital gowns my kids are wearing. Just look at them! They're scared shitless. But I still want a doctor to see them. What else did those monsters do? They put their hands on my children." His gaze was rigid and unmoving.

Raul glanced over to the kids, unusually quiet, eating their sandwiches, not happy or carefree like they should have been. When he glanced back to Asher, he saw the torment he was struggling with.

Asher ran his hands roughly through his wavy hair. "You hear me?" he said. "We're going as soon as they finish, and then you're telling me everything you saw, exactly where my kids were, and I want the names of everyone involved in putting those marks on my kids, touching them, doing God knows what to them. I may be a God-fearing man, but I want vengeance, Raul. There can be no mercy for the kinds of monsters who do this."

Raul didn't say a word. He wondered whether Asher would even have heard him.

"How could this happen? Damn it, I have so many questions. Why was Lydia there with our kids? How did she leave here and end up there? I feel sick, thinking they were gone all this time, my kids and Lydia. But they were in that place Wyatt stumbled upon. And I told you not to go! I'm so grateful you didn't listen." His brother had whispered the words, but every one dripped with angst.

Raul held his brother's gaze. "Yet you won't listen to me now."

Asher turned back to his kids, still standing beside Raul. "I'm hearing you, but I'm their father, and by God, if those people are waiting, as you say, to snatch them, they'll have to go through me. Now let's go. They're going to the hospital, and a doctor is going to look at them. Then I want the sheriff called. I want every law agency in the state to rain down on them the fires of hell. What I'm not going to do is hide out here. If you say they're coming for my kids, what's to stop them from coming here now?"

He hadn't expected such logic from Asher.

His brother nodded with finality and rested his hand on Raul's shoulder. "You drive," he said. "They're done, and as you've said, time's ticking."

Raul pulled his keys from his pocket and stepped out onto the porch, looking down at his dog, waiting till Asher followed him out, carrying both girls, little Arlis walking behind him. All were still in those hospital gowns, barefoot and quiet.

"You stay here, boy," Raul said to Dawg as he pulled the inside door closed and let the screen slap shut. "We'll be back soon."

Asher was already at his pickup, putting the kids inside. His truck was their only option, as Asher's older model, no bigger than his, had the hood up and a bucket under it.

"Raul, let's go!" Asher called out as he climbed in the truck and lifted Pearlie on his lap.

As Raul stepped off the porch and started walking to his pickup, he just hoped to all hell that he was wrong and the hospital would be safe, and no one would be waiting. But he suspected that kind of wishful thinking was exactly what the secret organization would be counting on.

THE SMELL OF HOSPITALS HAD ALWAYS LEFT HIM FEELING drained. It was the cleaning products and sterility mixed with something else, the abundance of drugs, the people and their emotions. He took in the doctors, nurses, and other staff milling in the corridor of the community hospital, a three-story building made of concrete and steel, only a few years old, replacing the old relic of a wood single-story building that had started out with eight rooms, a kitchen, and a small emergency room. It had been built, he figured, in the 1920s on land donated by one of the founding families in the area, whose name appeared on everything.

Raul sat on a padded bench where he could watch the emergency room and the doors to where his brother's kids were, and Asher too. He'd heard the whispers from the staff and knew social services had been called. Maybe it was unease that had him staying right where he was on that lone bench, his vantage point, so he could see who was coming and going. A woman in faded green scrubs walked out of the exam room his brother was in with the kids, followed by an older man in a white doctor's coat. Both were walking his way.

"Mr. Booth?" the older man asked.

Raul was already standing. "Raul, yes, Raul Booth."

The man was taller than the woman, about the same height as Raul. "I'm Doctor Rathwell, the head of psychiatry," he said, "and this is Doctor Penny." He gestured to the younger woman. Her hair was black but dyed with streaks of white and pink. Both were watching him seriously, which was rather fitting, considering the scenario. "Your brother, Asher, asked us to talk with you about what happened to the kids. Just so you know, social services have been called, and the sheriff's office has been alerted."

Of course they had. He wondered whether he made a face as he pulled his arms over his chest and lifted the flat of his hand, motioning for Dr. Rathwell to stop. "I know how the system works, and I also know what a knee-jerk reaction looks like. I'm assuming my brother told you I found the children."

"Your brother told a nonsensical story of a government town and a secret lab experimenting on them," Dr. Penny cut in sharply. "Absolute nonsense. You know, there's an expectation that parents should be stable, not spouting conspiracies. I don't believe it. As I said to Dr. Rathwell, your brother needs to be seen by a psychiatrist and assessed for his parental fitness. It will be up to social services to investigate what happened to those kids, but my recommendation will be for them to be placed somewhere safe until he is deemed not a threat."

This was worse than Raul had expected. "I'm sorry, who are you?" he said more calmly than he could have hoped. "Dr. Penny, was it, and you're how many years out of medical school? Rather green, I expect."

In his peripheral, two sheriff's deputies stood at the nurses' desk in the emergency room. Of course, they were there because of his brother's kids, his brother, and him.

"Two years," Dr. Penny said, "but that is irrelevant. I've worked the emergency room rotation for the last year—"

"And, let me guess, you believe you've seen everything, and once you form an opinion, there's no changing your mind. You took one look at my brother's kids and figured he did something, that he shaved their heads, tattooed barcodes on them—and then showed up here at the emergency room? To me, that doesn't make a lick of sense. If he did it, why would he bring them here?"

She pulled back, ready to argue with him.

"I think what Dr. Penny is saying," Dr. Rathwell cut in, "is that when we see children come in the condition of your nieces and nephew, questions have to be asked, hard questions."

Raul shook his head, lifting his hand again. "I would expect nothing less, but how about we set aside what you think you've figured out and take a step back. You saw the barcodes tattooed on the backs of their heads. Have you ever seen anything like that?" Raul said, addressing the head of psychiatry. He hoped, because of the man's age, he might not be as closeminded.

"People who hurt children are capable of just about anything," he said.

"Mr. Booth, with all due respect," Dr. Penny said, "do you really expect us to believe this ludicrous story about a lab experimenting and tattooing barcodes on those children? I'm sorry, but that's too farfetched for me. I may be young, but I'm not stupid. And before you try to convince me, you can sell it to the sheriff's deputies and social services. I'm just looking out for the children's welfare."

Raul wondered whether she could be reasoned with. How many children had been ripped away from their parents because of the opinions formed by this very young yet very arrogant doctor?

"I get that you're outraged," Raul said, "but park it, please, for the sake of those kids. Did you even take a look at them, physically, I mean? Please leave your disbelief and judgement behind for a moment and tell me how they are, because we have no idea what was done to them."

A man was walking their way, the sheriff's deputies hanging back outside the room his brother's kids were in. Shit, he knew what this was. They were standing guard so Asher couldn't leave with his children.

"I can take it from here, Dr. Penny," Dr. Rathwell said, holding up his hand to gesture for Raul to join him as he stepped aside. He suspected the younger doctor had been ready to argue but thought better of it.

"Of course," was all she said before walking back to the desk.

"Physically, the children appear fine," the head of psychiatry said. "I know some tests were run, blood and routine panels. Preliminary results have shown no traces of drugs, but what I'm concerned with is their mental state, the trauma. If what you've said is true, the trauma caused to those children can have prolonged, serious effects that could hinder their social development. You understand psychology? Your brother mentioned you used to be in the military, special forces."

Raul knew Asher would never talk about what he did,

because he didn't know everything. "I'm also a former deputy, law enforcement, so yeah, I understand what you're talking about." He had glanced out towards the men in the waiting room but turned now to face Dr. Rathwell again. "Let's cut to it. I'm not expecting you to believe me, but you can't be so naive as not to know that experiments on children and others have been carried out over the years, sanctioned by three-letter government agencies, nonprofits, and corporations for a variety of ends and reasons."

The head psychiatrist seemed rather calm. The way he was watching him, Raul wondered whether he had already labeled him crazy. "And you're saying this is one of those cases?"

He knew when someone was trying to manage him. "How about you just level with me? There are two deputies posted outside the room where the kids are—and who is that walking our way, a social worker or someone else?" Raul said. The man was dark haired, wearing a dark jacket and blue jeans. Raul turned to him before the psychiatrist could answer. "I presume you're looking for me, Raul Booth. Which agency are you with?"

The man didn't smile and didn't hold out his hand. "Thank you, Dr. Rathwell, but I have it from here," was all the man said as he pulled a card from his inside jacket pocket. "Jack Dole, from DCS."

Dr. Rathwell took the card. "Sure, just have me paged when you're done. Have you seen the children?"

"Not yet, but I will next. I just would like a word with Mr. Booth." Dole offered a tight smile, and the psychiatrist walked away. Something about the man unsettled Raul.

"DCS, really?" he said. "Now, why don't I believe you? Tell me, it's just you and me here. What agency are you really with? You think you're going to walk out of here with my brother's kids? I warned Asher as soon as we walked in here that someone would be dispatched. Tell me, did your phone ring as soon as someone entered the kids' names in the system here?"

Dole glanced once over his shoulder and then back to him. "Just who are you?" he said, unsmiling. There was an authority about him that bothered Raul.

"You know who I am, who my friends are," Raul said. "You grabbed the wrong kids. One call and I can find out who you are, too." He pulled out his cell phone.

The smile the man flashed his way now was cold, unfeeling. "Tell me, was your brother even looking for them?"

The statement caught him off guard. "So you target those you believe have no one to care for them, no one to search for them?"

His gaze was repulsive, a look Raul had seen far too many times before. "Scant resources in that area," Dole said. "Ask yourself, who listens to a poor man with nothing? But, apparently, someone didn't take you into account." He reached into his jacket pocket for his cell phone, which had buzzed. "Yeah?" was all he said into it, keeping his eyes fixed on Raul. "You sure?" He turned away.

The one-sided conversation was likely with someone important, Raul figured.

Dole hung up and turned back to him. "Looks like you've caught a break," he said, then tapped Raul's chest with his phone. "I'll give you some friendly advice. Just forget what you saw and go home. You got the kids. Consider that a gift."

Then he motioned to the deputies, who turned and left,

and Raul watched in disgust as the government agent walked past him and out the front door. Dole had known all too well that Asher hadn't been looking for his family. What bothered him most was the feeling that Lydia and the kids ending up in that town may not have been an accident.

CHAPTER 17

Smoke trailed just above the tree line as Raul drove back into Asher's place and parked. Harley was already there, waiting on the porch with his dog.

Asher was a big man, holding both girls on his lap, Arlis sitting between them on the bench seat. No one had said anything since they left the hospital, where the kids had been poked and prodded. A bottle of pills the psychiatrist insisted the kids would need was tucked in Asher's shirt pocket.

"Who's that?" Asher asked rather sharply, on edge. Harley was stepping off the porch, smoke rising from the chimney behind her.

"That would be Harley," Raul said. "She was with me in the town and went after Lydia…" But he didn't finish, as the screen door opened and Lydia stepped out. Asher was already out of the truck, and the kids too, calling out, "Mama, Mama!"

Lydia was running and in Asher's arms, crying, and the older two were there as well, hugging their dad. Harley walked right past them, past her Jeep, parked just at the side of the house, and toward him. The screen door squeaked, and Robin stepped out of the house, too, but stayed on the porch. By the way he was watching the family, Raul suspected there was more he needed to know.

"How long have you been here?" he said as Harley stopped in front of him, unsmiling.

"Not long. Thought I told you to stay away from the hospital. Robin could have had a look at them." She fisted her hands and pulled her arms over her chest, agitation rolling off her in waves. She blew out a breath.

"Did my best, but Asher wasn't having any of it," Raul said. "See what they did to the kids—shaved their heads, tattooed them with barcodes? You were right, though. It didn't take long for them to show up at the hospital. Only thing I can't figure out is who called them off."

Asher had pulled his eldest two into his arms as they started back to the house. They and Lydia still had all their hair, so it was just the little ones who had been cataloged.

His dog had come to sit beside him. Raul leaned down and hugged him, giving him a good rub. "God damn, I missed you, Dawg."

Harley shook her head as he stood up. "Can only figure we made enough noise, and they likely hadn't counted on you. What did the doctor say? How are they?" She turned, gesturing to the house, where Asher was holding the screen door open for his family. Robin was saying something to Asher, and both looked over at them.

"Physically, the kids are fine," Raul said. "They didn't find any drugs in their systems, although they've lost weight. The shrink gave Asher some psychotropic drugs that he said would help the kids, but I told him not to do it, as the effects will likely be worse. After what his kids have been through, turning them into zombies isn't a solution. No idea what trauma they endured, what nightmares will come. Arlis said they were sat in front of a TV for hours alone, watching a man talking, then a woman. He didn't elaborate, and Asher wouldn't push. I wanted to, but Asher said leave him be. He's scared. My brother has never seen him like this. Can't blame him."

The face Harley made had him pausing. She squinted into the distance as if gathering her thoughts and then nodded. "Lydia remembers nothing, and I mean nothing," she said. "She's confused, didn't know who she was until I showed her that picture of her, the kids, and Asher. She had no idea why she was in the mall. It was like a switch flicked, and then only bits and pieces of her memory came back. She was mumbling under her breath; it was disconcerting. The older two we found with a group of teens, all dressed the same, in orange shirts and blue jeans. They sat like robots—and I'm not kidding, fucking robots, saying nothing and looking straight ahead the entire way back. Robin tried talking to them."

She gave her head a shake. "I'm sorry, Raul. This sucks, what they did, and worse is not knowing the details. Robin mentioned something about a treatment called depatterning to break the mind down. It includes drugging, putting the victim in a coma, breaking down the mind to a childlike state, and then reprogramming, playing recorded messages for up to twenty hours a day whether asleep or awake. Not a hundred percent sure, though, as Lydia seems confused every time I bring up the town and why she left Asher. How did she end up there? What happened there? It's as if she can't remember anything. Robin has offered to stay a few days, Raul, and I think that would be a good idea. Talk to Asher, convince him." She was looking right at him now, the seriousness of the situation really setting in.

"Don't think I'll need to convince him of that," Raul said. "He'll welcome the help."

It was so quiet there in the hills, he thought, only the peace had changed into something sinister.

"Raul, while we waited for you, Robin asked Lydia and the older ones for some water. Lydia didn't know how to turn on the tap. He said he's pretty sure she's been subjected to electroshock treatments. The two kids, he's not sure. You're going to need help for them, and you may never know what happened to all of them down in that lab. You want my guess on the little ones with the barcodes?"

Raul wasn't sure he did, because he feared it would be what he was already thinking.

"They were likely to be shipped off, loaded into a cargo container, and sold for any number of purposes—organs, blood, slavery, test subjects, and likely more heinous fates that I haven't thought of."

He met her gaze, and the grimness lingered between them. "Their hair will grow back, but the barcodes will always be there as a reminder," he said. "I'll be sticking around for a while to help Asher. What about the congressman, the mall explosion?"

"Best I can figure is their plan was foiled. Was it because of us?" She let her hands fall and gestured helplessly. "I have no idea. Jeffrey stayed behind to meet up with Chogan at some point. Before I left, I made some calls and pulled every string I could to have a word with the congressman, who had already been hauled out of there by his security. Unfortunately, it wasn't face to face, but at least I talked to him over the phone. I'm not sure he believed me about the town, but I told him everything. There were guns stashed in duffle bags found under the stage in the mall. All I can figure is our showing up stopped whatever had been planned, whatever role those from the town had to play. Could there have been a mass shooting, casualties? Were Lydia and the older ones to play a part? I don't know, because Lydia doesn't remember anything.

"All I know is it didn't work. We messed up their plans, and that has likely put a target on all of us. The whole area is crawling with cops and federal agents now. I suspect the media spin on what happened at the mall opening will be something else entirely. Early reports are saying it was an explosion that could be tied to faulty workmanship. No mention of the guns found, or the explosion being from a planted device, or any hint that it was a possible assassination attempt on the congressman. The early news reports are being downplayed." She let out a heavy sigh. "I put a call in to my boss, as well. I expect the congressman has already called everyone and anyone about the little town that doesn't exist. I plan on heading back now." Harley appeared uneasy.

"You want to be part of it, don't you?" he said. "The good guys going in and taking the bad guys down."

She didn't smile, but there was a hint of something, sadness mixed with the same sense of justice he felt. "Would be lying if I said no. I've done all I can here, brought Lydia and the kids back. Robin, this is his area. He'll stay and help, but I'm going to head back. I don't want to miss the action." She tapped his arm and started walking over to her Jeep.

"Hey, Harley…" Raul glanced over to the house, where his dog was waiting on the porch for him. Harley stopped and watched him curiously. "I think I'll tag along with you."

She looked over to the house. "What about your family?"

"As you said, Robin's here, and Lydia and the kids are safe, but I've still got business in that town. I still need answers about Wyatt. After all, if it hadn't been for him and his sacrifice, stumbling upon that town, I never would have found Lydia and the kids, and my brother would likely always have believed she'd run off."

CHAPTER 18

Standing by his pickup, parked on the side of a stretch of road behind Harley's Jeep, Raul stared out at nothing but dirt and concrete and some trees in the distance, all that was left of what had once been a pretty little town called Shadow Valley. "Holy shit, how is this possible?" he said. "Are we in the right place?"

Harley, staring off into the distance, shook her head. "Cleanup on aisle six," she said. It was an odd comment that had come out of nowhere. She shrugged, glancing back at him. "Sorry, bad sense of humor. Seems no one was supposed to see this. I'm just having a little trouble wrapping my head around how you make a town disappear. All the buildings that were here, even the town square—the only thing left is this little bit of cobblestone." She kicked dirt covering the patch of stone that hadn't been heaped with a small mountain of gravel. He kicked away some of the dirt, too, and saw more of the cobblestone underneath.

"No clock tower, no buildings, no people. Even the sign for Shadow Valley is gone," he said. "Tell me, who has the kind of power to make this all go away? Think of the manpower that would be needed to take buildings down, cover up the roads and sidewalks. You made a call to your boss, and then there's the congressman and the calls he made. How many agencies would have been alerted, all with the resources to pull this off?" He was so pissed, but he couldn't get past how calm he sounded. "Come on, Harley. This is rather convenient, isn't it? You called your boss and who else? There's no one here but you and me. What the fuck is going on?"

"Hey," she said rather sharply. Fire flashed in her amber eyes. "I'm just as thrown as you, so don't go accusing me of being part of this cleanup!"

"Well, you are CIA. Isn't the motto, 'Be covert and lie your ass off'? Come to think of it, are you playing a role, pretending you're someone you're not so you can mislead, misdirect, infiltrate? Is that what this is? Are you infiltrating, and for what means? I don't understand what the fuck you're doing, Harley."

He didn't see it coming—the fist in his face that had him stumbling. He lifted his hand to his jaw.

She shook her hand as if she'd hurt it, shaking it out, spewing with anger. "You asshole! Don't you ever accuse me of being disloyal, a spy, or part of this after I went after your family and brought them back! The rug has been yanked out from under me, too. Parts of the CIA may be doing bad things, and we all know it, but there are still a few of us trying to make a difference. Don't you accuse me of lying!" She made a rude noise under her breath and gestured sharply at him.

Just then, Raul's cell phone rang. He pulled it out and didn't recognize the number. "Hello?" he said, fury still staring back at him from a woman who had way too many secrets.

"I suppose you've probably already figured out that the town is gone," a man with a deep voice said.

"Chief Walker?" It couldn't be. He took in Harley's frown, the way her brow furrowed as she watched him.

"Walker will do, as the chief part is pretty much done."

"It's not your real name, though, is it?"

There was silence on the other end for a moment. "Is that what you really want to ask me?"

Raul already knew it was a moot point. It had all been a role he was playing, but why? "No, I guess not. How about why you're calling me, how you got my number? How can a town disappear in less than a day? Who do you work for, really? What experiments were going on here with my brother's kids? What was the plan? Who killed my friend Wyatt and put him in a motel room two hundred miles away? Let's start there."

Harley was still watching him. Above the horizon, the sun dipped lower.

"You have a lot of questions, Raul Booth. You should be happy you walked out of here with your brother's kids and that your friends found his wife the way they did. I'm sure your brother will be happy with the compensation that will be offered. Oh, of course, he'll be required to sign a government nondisclosure agreement—a standard one that will bring life imprisonment and losing everything if he talks. But it will be enough that he'll be able to bring some comfort to his wife, who won't remember anything, and the five kids. Enough that he can move them from that shack in the hills to a nice place in the city, a fresh new start somewhere he can get help for them. Enough to start over and be comfortable with the thanks of Uncle Sam. Tell him to take the money.

"Your friend Wyatt almost got away—almost. Heard he was a hard one to track. He saw something he wasn't supposed to see. Someone got sloppy, and Wyatt walked right in. Orders were given to clean up and dispose of the body. Just to save you some time, his death will be ruled an accidental overdose by the fentanyl found in his system. Bags have already been discovered in the small cabin where he lived, planted, of course. The case is closed. And the entrances underground have been permanently sealed."

He shook his head and turned back to Harley. "The congressman knows about this town and what was planned…"

"Rollins knows shit," Walker cut Raul off rather sharply. "This is way above his paygrade, and right about now, he's likely been convinced that a few nutjobs spun this wild tale of a town not on the map, with an underground lab, to make him look like a fool, embarrass him. I expect he has already been advised the place doesn't exist. He's moved on to dealing with the accident at the mall. It's being called shoddy construction, and the congressman may have ties to the contractor behind the build. See how it works? They figured out another angle after you messed up their plan. At least they found a way to take the congressman out. I expect the news will report on the favors exchanged, the money that changed hands, and the bribes the congressman was taking. All untrue, of course, but that won't matter. He'll never get ahead of it. The spin doctors are already out in front. You may want to keep a low profile, too, Mr. Booth. Tell your friends to forget what they think they saw. This is one web that is out of all of your reach, including that rogue CIA girl standing next to you."

An icy chill ran through Raul, his heart pounding, and he looked around, turning frantically in a circle. "You're watching us. Where are you?"

Harley stiffened and turned around quickly, looking into the distance and then back to him, gesturing, her eyes wide.

"Doesn't matter where I am. Anything you have, any evidence you found, you won't be able to show it to anyone. You think we don't know one of you was in the computer mainframe and downloaded details of the Black Mountain Project? Top secret, of course. That can never be used. The girl knows that. Did you know that experimental location was in operation for fifteen years? The data collected will never be seen by the public. Go home and back to your family, Raul."

"I don't understand any of this. How did you get Lydia, the kids? She left Asher. Did they drive in here by accident? And why did you help me get them out? I know you did!"

"You have a lot of questions, but I don't have much time left, and neither do you. A family alone, a woman with kids who has left her husband, was easy to spot. People are in trouble all the time, especially when they have barely enough to get by. There are watchers out there everywhere who see them, offer them help. Next they're on a bus, or in the back of a van, or in a trunk. Taken is taken. Your brother's family was found outside a fast-food restaurant, counting change to feed the kids, with suitcases in the back of the car. A stranger stopped for a friendly chat. It's amazing how many will freely share their personal information. Lydia was told of a new town offering families a free place to stay, with some jobs, good schools. Exactly what she was looking for. But now it's time for you and me to go. Have a great life. Look after that family. Tick-tock, Raul. You two need to get in your vehicles and drive out of here. Nothing left for you to see."

Then the line went dead, and Raul found himself looking into the hills, past Harley, and then at her.

"What was that about?" she said.

"He's watching us," he said. "Guess I owe you an apology."

For a second, she said nothing, still pissed. "You do, Raul, to be clear. Now, what do you want to bet that when I call my boss again, I'll be told to stand down."

He didn't know what to say to that. Just then, his phone rang again, his brother's name on the screen this time. "Asher, hey. I'm on my way back."

"Raul, some lawyer just showed up here, wanting to pay me two million for what happened to my family. He says he's from the government and wants me to sign some papers so I can't talk about where I got the money or anything about Lydia and the kids or where they were, the experiments that were done. I want answers. I'm not a fool, Raul. This is hush money."

There it was, the payoff. He let the phone slip from his mouth. He hadn't expected it to come this fast. "Asher, I know you want answers, but I need you to trust me here and sign it. Take the money. You'll need it for the kids, for Lydia. Take it, because you can't talk to anyone about this anyway, not right now."

Harley, watching him, made a face. He had to turn away.

"Why would I do that?" Asher said. "Yes, this is a lot of

money, Raul, but I'm not okay with someone paying me because they hurt my kids, my wife."

He jammed his hand in his hair, turning back to Harley, who was looking out into the forested hills again. "I'm not, either, but this isn't about that. Look, Asher, I need you to trust me on this. Justice will come, and there will be a time for it, but not if you're dead or if Lydia and the kids are suddenly disappeared. Trust me, please, sign it. Take the money." He pressed his thumb and forefinger to the bridge of his nose, hearing the sigh on the other end.

"You're my brother, Raul. If you tell me to trust you, I do. Are you sure about this?"

He shook his head. "Not really, but do it anyway. I'm on my way home."

"All right, then. I hope you're right about this."

Asher hung up, and Raul pocketed his phone. That left just him and Harley.

"They sent someone to pay your brother off," Harley said matter-of-factly.

"Quick, aren't they?" He started back to his pickup, Harley right beside him.

"They're cleaning up. Guess that means they'll leave them be."

He really hoped she was right as he walked around to the driver's side and pulled open his door, looking back into the hills. "Walker is still here, watching us. What do you think he's about—good, bad, or just fucking with us?"

"You want my two cents?" She'd already pulled open the door of her Jeep ahead of him.

"Why not?"

"Maybe he was playing us. Maybe whatever was going on here was done, and it was time to move on, so he tossed us a few crumbs because the plan had changed anyway. Or maybe he had a conscience after all. Or maybe it's none of that, and he's undercover to bring the house of cards down. What I can tell you is he's an agency guy, but which one, I have no idea. We should go."

This wasn't the happy ending he'd expected. No justice, none of the answers he wanted, and a truth he was not comfortable with. He looked over his shoulder again. "You'll follow me back to Asher's?" he said. He'd have given anything to know what she was thinking.

"I'll be right behind you."

CHAPTER 19

Walker watched through his binoculars as the pickup and Jeep pulled out of what was left of the town. Dump trucks full of dirt had covered the paved roads and cobblestone walkways, turning the area into nothing more than a gravel pit. He waited from the side of the hill, just off the trail, as Raul and the girl he'd been warned about wound their way into the distance, with no signs of anyone else around.

"Sir, can we blow it now?"

Walker handed the binoculars to one of the soldiers, a Sergeant First Class. Walker couldn't remember his name. It wasn't important to him. He glanced at his watch, noting it was already past five. Everything in the labs would be gone in minutes, leaving nothing of the facility that had cost billions to build.

"Is the chopper here?" someone asked.

Walker turned to see Sergeant Major Johnson, a covert team leader from the US Army Special Operations Unit. There were only four, including the newest one, who had been with the team for only eight months. Walker was the only one not armed.

"Waiting," he said. "Time to go. Six minutes and counting, and I'd just as soon not be anywhere near here. Let's move."

He felt a weight lift, knowing Raul Booth was now gone. Johnson fell in beside him, and the helicopter rotors started up with a whir.

"All those kids are safe?" Walker said. It wasn't something he usually asked, maybe because he'd been doing this for too long.

"All located, and most have been reunited with their families," Johnson said. "A few, we don't know where they came from, but they'll be looked after, sir." He had his hand on Walker's shoulder, urging him forward as the wind whipped up around them. They both ducked as Johnson hurried him onto the helicopter, helping him up as the other four leaped in. He had just buckled in when the helicopter lifted off.

"Did you get everyone?" asked Master Sergeant Williams, a redhead, who watched him with a coldness that made him look away, back over to Johnson, beside him.

"Most of the lab techs, a few of the doctors," Johnson said. "Some they can't touch, and the rest are in the wind."

It had been a cryptic response, as if Johnson hadn't been too interested. Then the explosion underground sent dust flying, and the chopper moved past the hills. Looking back through the open door at the size of the explosion, Walker knew there would be nothing left underground.

"So how long were you down there?" Williams asked.

"Two years too long," Walker replied. Again, he had to look away.

"Doesn't it bother you, watching them and doing nothing while innocent people are experimented on, killed? I don't know how you do it."

So Williams thought he was a monster.

"Someone has to so that we can end this," Walker said. "It's called acting, playing a role. You may not like what I do, but it's not that different from the orders you've had to follow. How many times in the past were you sent in to eliminate a hostile only to discover it was the other way around, that you were the enemy and your target had become a threat to whatever government agenda was being worked behind the scenes? With all due respect, I think I'll sleep better tonight knowing the Black Mountain Project and Shadow Valley are one more black site that's been taken off the map."

Williams smiled and said, "Amen, brother. Amen."

As the helicopter soared away from the now obliterated site, Walker felt a complex mix of relief and foreboding. Beneath him, the secrets of Shadow Valley and its dark undertakings had dissolved into history, leaving a narrative only he and a select few would ever fully understand. This mission was over, but the echo of its consequences would resonate long after the dust had settled.

Turn the page for a sneak peek of
THE SACRIFICE
Available in print, eBook & audio

DISCOVER THE ORIGINS OF RAUL BOOTHE: READ "THE SACRIFICE"

Meet Raul Boothe as he steps into the pivotal role of small town deputy, filling the shoes of the legendary Mark Friessen. Dive into the gripping narrative that started it all in "The Sacrifice." Are you ready to uncover the beginnings of a hero?

THE SACRIFICE

Chief Mark Friessen is about to be a family man, with a baby on the way. However, he faces a choice: Either he breaks his word to his wife by taking on a job that will put him in danger, or he stays silent, which would haunt him forever.

Mark lives and dies by his word, and he would do anything for his wife but park his morals and turn his back on those he has sworn to protect, kids and animals, a promise he made to his wife and to himself.

After evidence uncovers a global child trafficking network with ties to his island, Mark is contacted by a secret agency of retired servicemen and cops who ask him to help track down and rescue the children no one is looking for.

The only problem is that Billy Jo is pregnant, and accepting the mission will mean Mark needs to leave her for weeks or months on end. As he struggles with his decision to leave the job he loves and the island that has become his home, he realizes he's at a crossroads. He will need to give everything to save the children, bringing an end to the trafficking of minors, and the elite who prey on them, forever. It's the only way to bring everyone involved to justice.

Yet the kids he's trying to save are not the only ones in danger. When a phone call from home brings everything full circle, Mark's ultimate sacrifice could be Billy Jo and his unborn baby.

THE SACRIFICE
CHAPTER 1

There was something about the fall, the cool mornings, the days becoming shorter. It seemed everything was preparing for the cold that would soon be upon them. Mark listened to the crackle of wood as he started the early-morning fire in the woodstove to take the chill out of the air.

Still barefoot after pulling on blue jeans and a navy sweatshirt, he heard the familiar sound of Billy Jo's three-legged cat, Harley, munching on kibble. Lucky, his mutt, and Sarge, a light lab, appeared at the sliding glass door, evidently ready to come in, too. He walked over to the door and opened it, taking in the quiet. He'd left his wife sound asleep.

"That was quick this morning," he said to his dogs. The wind was cold, and the rain was just holding off. A light frost, the first of the season, covered the grass.

A door downstairs clicked, and footsteps came up the stairs just as the coffeemaker beeped. "Good morning, Mark," Gail said, pulling at the tie of her pale green robe, wearing slippers and flannel pajama pants. She leaned down and gave Lucky and Sarge a good petting as Mark filled two dog bowls with kibble.

"Good morning, Gail," he said. "Coffee's ready."

"Oh, I see you started the fire," she said. "Think I'll park myself in front of it with coffee this morning. You know, I feel spoiled, Mark. I get up in the morning and you have coffee ready and the house warm. But I've been thinking I can't live here forever. There's a point where I'll need to go home." She turned over one of the four matching green floral mugs that Billy Jo loved, which were sitting beside the coffeemaker, clean and ready. That was just something his wife did. "You get a coffee yet?" Gail asked as she poured hers in the mug.

"No, not yet," he said. "Pour me one, too, please."

Mark put both dog dishes down on the other side of the island, away from the cat, as Gail filled another mug and set it down there for him. "I take it Billy Jo is still asleep," she said.

"No, I'm awake, and I can smell the coffee. Please pour me one, too," Billy Jo said, emerging from the bedroom. She was in a long nightshirt and wool socks, her blue fluffy housecoat pulled on but wide open over her swollen six-month belly. It appeared for a moment as if the baby had grown overnight. Damn, she was a beautiful sight.

"You sleep okay?" he said.

She was still yawning as Gail walked over to her and handed her a coffee. Mark let his gaze linger as he waited for her to take a swallow and answer him.

"Only had to get up once to go to the bathroom," she said, "but I have to say we can add the spaghetti to the list of meals we'll skip until after the baby is born. Too heavy, and it left me with a lingering heartburn. Oh, and I got a text from Lisa just now, which is what woke me after I finally settled into a deep sleep, a dream I now can't remember." She pulled her cellphone from the pocket of her housecoat and handed it to him, something he hadn't expected.

"You need to tell her to stop texting so early, or I will," he said.

She only rolled her eyes and walked to the living room, from which he could already feel the heat of the woodstove. "Just read it, Mark, and stop nagging. Important is important."

Mark took a swallow of the steaming coffee and typed in his wife's passcode, then took in the text from Lisa:

Just checked messages at the office about the Palmer kid, Mila. DCFS returned her to her mother last night, but Mom wants to know what happened to her daughter, as she has a red medical incision on her abdomen, left side. I pulled up the file, but nothing shows.

Another text dinged: *Scratch that. Mom is on the warpath. She's at the ER right now. Got a call from the ER doc because Mom has threatened half the staff after they discovered her daughter's left kidney was removed. They want us to go down and take daughter from her. Do I go?*

Mark just stared. He could feel Billy Jo watching him as he squeezed the phone, and he flicked his gaze to her. She lifted her brows, blowing on her mug of steaming coffee, and said nothing. At what point would he need to yank his wife from this cesspool of the DCFS? Stress was stress, and he still couldn't believe she wasn't all over this.

Mark let his gaze linger on Gail and Billy Jo in the living room, his wife now in the leather recliner and Gail adding another piece of wood to the fire. A knock at the door had them both looking his way, and he took in the clock on the stove, which read 7:15 a.m.

"Yeah, I'll get it," was all he said. He put his coffee down beside Billy Jo's phone and strode to the front door, feeling that unease that seemed to build every day and never leave. He flicked the deadbolt, and Lucky was already right beside him, letting out a woof. Sarge quickly followed, barking more.

"Quiet down," Mark said before he pulled open the door and took in two tall men, one in a dark coat, the other a light brown. Something about them screamed Fed, and he spotted the familiar bulge of a sidearm under each of their coats. No badges, but everything about them, the way they stood, the way they stared at him, said enough. He let his gaze linger on their clean-shaven faces and two black SUVs parked behind his Jeep. There were three more men in his driveway, one by the side of the house, wearing dark clothes, and one in military fatigues, watching, standing guard.

What the hell? His heart thudded, and he thought of his gun tucked inside his gun safe in the bedroom. Sloppy. "Can I help you?"

"Are you Mark Friessen?"

He didn't turn around even when he heard footsteps behind him. "Mark, who is it?" Billy Jo said. Damn, why couldn't she stay put? There was the cold fear he recognized and never wanted to feel again.

"Billy Jo, take Lucky and Sarge. Stay in the house." He knew it had come out rather sharply, and he glanced only once to Billy Jo and his baby growing inside her, seeing the moment she understood.

"Come on, you two." She reached for Sarge's collar, then Lucky's, and pulled them back down the hall.

Mark stepped out of the house, barefoot, feeling the chill in the air. He pulled the door closed and wished again that he had his gun. He didn't like being caught off guard. "Who are you, military? Why are you at my house?"

The one at his door, dark hair, close cropped, about Mark's height and build, gestured to him. "Would like to have a word with you," he said. "Wondering if we could talk over here."

He realized it wasn't a question, as the other guy was already down the stairs. Mark took in the security camera outside, which still had to be hooked up, and followed them both down to the side of the house. They walked as if they knew exactly where they were going, and the hair rising at the back of his neck was just another warning about how vulnerable he and his family were. Everything in him was screaming, *What the fuck?*

"Okay, you have me here at the side of my house," he said. "Who the hell are you?" He couldn't make out the other two guys by the vehicle, but he had a feeling they were special forces, maybe. It was just something about the way they stood, the way they were positioned to the side, as if each had a job.

"We're with the military," the dark-haired man said. "We've been following you, Chief Friessen, and we've put together a special unit going after human traffickers, child traffickers. We'd like you to join our team."

He just stared. For a second, he couldn't come up with a reasonable response. "What?" He glanced between the two men. The other was chewing a piece of gum and glancing everywhere but at Mark. He had a mustache, light brown hair, and was a few inches shorter. These men were not desk jockeys, judging by how pumped they appeared, from weights and training or something. "I'm not clear," he said. "You're with the US military?"

"No, not entirely US," said the dark-haired one,

jumping in, and Mark picked up something in his accent that said he wasn't from around there.

"Look, boys, I need a little more than what you're giving me," he said. "I'm not entirely comfortable with you showing up at my door, either. My family is here. You say you're not entirely US, so what does that mean, exactly?"

The shorter one with light-brown hair and a mustache dragged his gaze over Mark. His eyes were brown, and the edge in them gave nothing away. "We can't disclose too much," he said. "Let's just say we're a team comprising some former military, some current military, former law enforcement, and former intelligence from the US and a few other countries. What we're doing is putting together a team to put an end to trafficking on a worldwide scale. Right now, I'm sure you're aware human trafficking was once surpassed by guns and drugs, but there's more to it, and we can't say too much unless we get a commitment from you to join our team. We operate under the radar, but we're tackling head-on something that has remained untouchable."

Mark let out a rough laugh, which, he realized, was likely not what they'd expected. He jammed his hands through his thick red hair. He didn't know what to think, and he wondered for a second whether this was a joke.

"I understand you may be a little thrown," the man said. "This is highly unusual, but we're in a different world now, Chief. Let me ask you something. You feel as if your hands are tied at times? We've been following you. We know about the trafficking ring you discovered on the island, the one the old chief was a part of, and the church minister who was a staple of the island. For how many decades have children been moved through here, under the radar? One of your cops was even part of it, and a prominent pediatrician, and how many on the town council were aware? This is only one island. You brought it down single-handedly, but you've found yourself in a constant political battle ever since. You've been looking into every resident of the island because you have a feeling this is bigger than you can imagine. You've battled constant red tape, district attorneys refusing to prosecute, working against you. You're up against a line of predators who can operate unscathed because of who they are and the power they hold. Then there was the social worker before your wife. How many kids disappeared, were trafficked and sold?"

"If I recall," Mark said, knowing he sounded pissed, "you guys showed up and took all the case files, shutting down my investigation into the kids the caseworker was responsible for, who basically disappeared. The missing money and all the evidence is gone."

The dark-haired one had the same expression as the other guy, a hardness that gave nothing away. "Not us," he said.

"It was the military." Mark leaned in, hearing the asshole tone of his voice. He didn't like being blown off.

"Chief, you can't be that naïve," the man said. "You know there are multiple branches within the military. Units follow the orders they're given and don't even realize that the people whose orders they're following aren't the ones they swore allegiance to. You were over the target, getting too close, and have stepped on toes. Others are watching you, too, not just us."

He thought his ears were ringing. "What? Who's watching me?" He found himself looking over his shoulder. The chill that went up his back bothered him in ways he couldn't have explained to anyone.

"Those whose toes you're stepping on. You don't want to be on their radar. Leaves you with that nice, tingly feeling, doesn't it? Maybe you want to sit with this for a minute. And that camera you have at the front door? You should get it hooked up."

Then both men turned and started walking back to the front.

"Wait," Mark called out. "I don't even know who you are, your names, how to get a hold of you. You just show up here and drop this bomb on me?"

The mustached man looked back to him, and Mark figured he was the one in charge. "You can call me Dion, but understand we didn't have this conversation. We'll give you a bit to think about what we're offering, what it is we're asking of you. Just know that it's best you don't share this with anyone. This isn't a job, Mark Friessen. We're asking you to join the team. There will be training. We're going after these traffickers, after the children. Some we can save, but many we can't. Think about it, Mark. How many children go missing every minute, never to be found again? Who's taking them? This is bigger than you think. We'll give you the morning."

"Wait," Mark said. "I have a wife and a baby on the way."

Dion didn't pull his gaze, which, for the first time, held something that resembled emotion. "Maybe that's another reason we're asking. Again, Mark, we've done our homework on you and your wife, the social worker. Billy Jo, is it?"

He liked this even less, these men he didn't know anything about bringing up his wife. "Who do you work for, then? Who funds you? Who do you report to? I kind of need to know more than what you've told me, just showing up here and asking me to join some task force. I'm the chief on this island. You're asking me to walk away from my job. Who is going to watch over the people here, keep things safe? The former chief wasn't part of it by choice, so you evidently know somebody got to him. My question, are those same somebodies watching me? I won't keep this from my wife. We have no secrets."

Dion gestured to him, standing at the front of the house now. There was no window at that side, and three tall, thick fir trees also sheltered them. They were out of view of everything. "You'll be briefed in full detail when you decide to join the team. You'll sign a military NDA. What you learn will be classified, and you can share only what isn't. You'll have to explain it to your wife. We have our own families, too, who understand that what we're doing is important. You can share the general gist, just not ops. Those details don't get released to anyone outside the team. I shouldn't have to explain why. Your chief was gotten to because the people responsible, who have you in their sight now, operate in the shadows and compromise those they can't buy, those like your former chief, among others."

How much did Mark really know about the intelligence community? Less than he should. For a second, as he stood there, he couldn't get his brain to come up with anything he knew he should be asking. "How do I get a hold of you?"

Dion only shook his head, then started walking, "We'll contact you," he called out over his shoulder.

Mark followed, stepping over the pinecones on the grass, and watched as five men climbed in two SUVs, backed out, and drove away. He took a second, standing in the cool morning air, unable to shake the feeling that he was now at a crossroads, and whatever choice he made would forever change his life.

It was unsettling. His wife was pregnant, but what was the thing he'd always promised her? Kids and animals, he'd sworn to protect them.

CHAPTER 2

Lucky had let out a soft woof as Mark headed out the front door, and he still sat there, waiting, whereas Sarge was already eating his kibble again.

"Lucky, come here, boy. Lie down," Billy Jo said, gesturing sharply to the dog bed in the corner of the living room.

Gail gave the dog a rub as he walked past her and over to his bed, but instead of lying, he sat. "He's just worried," she said. "Doesn't like it when he can't do his job, looking after Mark."

"Yeah, well, the feeling is mutual," Billy Jo said. "You see him out there?"

Gail shook her head, then walked over to the living room to look out the front window. "No, he's out of sight, and that's not a good thing. What do you think they want? Does Mark know them?" She was looking out into the back yard now.

Billy Jo couldn't shake her unease. She knew when Mark was on edge, worried, scared in a way that had him going all alpha like he had a few minutes earlier. It was just a look, his voice, and the tension she could feel coming off him in waves. "I know nothing," Billy Jo said. "That's the problem. I don't know who they are. I don't think Mark does, either, by the way he acted. He just told me to take the dogs."

She heard the door open and put her coffee mug down as she heard Mark's heavy footsteps. He appeared, his gaze intense, tension pulling across those broad shoulders and arms that held her every night.

He said nothing as he walked over to the island, where her phone and his coffee mug were, but instead of reaching for it, he seemed lost in thought.

"Mark, who was that?" she said. "Did you know them? What did they want?"

His hands were now resting on the edge of the island, and he leaned heavily on them before stepping back. How quiet he was in that second really bothered her.

"Mark, what's going on?"

He gave his head a shake. His red hair still had that bedhead look. "I don't know who they are," he said. "Some type of military unit. Special forces, from what I figure. Didn't really say. Didn't offer their names or where they're from, only this cloak and dagger shit. No, I don't know them, but they seem to know all about me."

Mark pushed away from the island, then reached for his mug and took a swallow of his coffee, but it was likely cold, as he walked over to the sink and dumped it out before reaching for the carafe to refill it. Billy Jo glanced over to Gail, who was still standing by the sliding glass door, wearing that motherly look as she watched Mark closely. Then she dragged her gaze to Billy Jo. Okay, so she had picked up on it, as well.

Mark didn't turn around, which had her suspecting

that what he said next would be something she wouldn't like. "You remember what happened here, what we found under the minister's house, under the floor?" he said. "The cells, the rooms where he was keeping kids? And the things he was doing with them, selling them? It's something no one wants in their head."

There it was again, that awful knot in her stomach. Mark turned around and let his gaze linger on her, and she could see in his amazing sky-blue eyes that there was way more. She could only nod as she pulled her lower lip between her teeth and instinctually rested her hands on her baby, the flutter of life that she felt throughout the day. Mark's gaze went right to the baby she carried, then over to Gail.

"They offered me a job," he said. "Actually, I don't think it's really a job. It's more that they want me to join a task force or something, considering what I found, that small pedophile ring hidden here. There appear to be many more. I don't even know who those guys are, but if what one of them said is true, they're former cops, military, intelligence..." Mark stopped talking, and she recognized the quiet place he went, seeming to hold on to things. He stared into his mug of coffee and then shook his head, making a face. "When I first became a deputy, I never expected to find what I did on this island. I've had my eyes opened in ways I never thought possible. I believed the world to be one way, but I'm starting to think everything I thought to be true was a lie. I knew deep down that the problem wasn't isolated to this island." He let his gaze linger, and she had an awful feeling of an impending change.

"So what does this mean, exactly, Mark?" she said. She knew Gail hadn't moved, just listening to everything.

"You have a job as the chief on this island. This is our home."

Mark's face told her everything he hadn't said, and it really hit home. "I think you know what it means. From the little they said, if I join this team, I won't be chief here anymore. That's all I know. It's military, but not what we think of. I don't know all the details. Seems they operate under the radar, which is the only way to go after the kind of corruption we're talking about. Drugs and illegal guns have been coming across our border, out of control, for so long, but human trafficking has exceeded everything. You know what I'm talking about—kids, babies, women. This is about taking them down, and that's all I know. I'll know the details only if I decide to join. Some things are classified, and no one outside the team can know. I think you already know that the people involved in trafficking are in positions of power. They have access to everything, and they have people everywhere."

Billy Jo put down her mug of coffee. "And why does it have to be you?"

He walked over to her after setting his own mug down and rested his hands on her shoulders, then ran them down over her arms so tenderly, lovingly. "I didn't say yes," he said. "They want me to think about it. Only if I commit to joining them will I know more. I'm not taking on something without talking to you. I'm telling you what I know and what they want. For all I know, this could be someone messing with me."

"I don't think you believe that, Mark," Gail cut in.

Billy Jo turned to her. Gail's expression was tense and heavy, and from the face she made, Billy Jo wondered whether she was thinking again of what Tolly had done. She didn't know how she'd feel if it had been Mark.

"We've never talked about what happened," Gail said, "not really. But think about it. Who has that kind of power, to have gotten to my husband through my son, having him agreeing to look the other way as innocent kids were preyed on? It wouldn't just be here. How many others are involved? How deep does this go, how far up the chain of command? The low-hanging fruit, the working class, is doing the dirty work, but how many are pulling the strings, controlling this? They have the power and money to control the system, so who has that kind of power?"

Billy Jo felt Mark squeeze her arm as if he needed to hold on to it.

"I think you and I both know we're talking at a level above governments," he said. "But, as I said, I haven't accepted anything, and I may not even hear from them again. Speaking of which, about that text from Lisa, I'll call her and handle it. I'm going to grab a shower and head in to work." He pressed a kiss to her forehead. "Why don't you stay home this morning, put your feet up and take it easy?" He let his fingers run gently down the side of her face.

"No, I'm right behind you," she said. "I have some files I need to clean up, calls to make, and I plan to be there when you have your chit-chat with Lisa. One thing I've learned about her is that she loves to go down the rabbit hole, finding things and digging in places the average person will never go, but it could be just another screwup."

He said nothing. For a second, she wondered whether he'd tell her no, but he just nodded and lingered there, and she pressed the flat of her hand to his chest. It was so instinctual to touch him. Then he was walking away, into the bedroom, and Billy Jo turned to Gail, who was shaking her head.

"Who do you think those men work for?" Billy Jo said. "The military? What do you think he meant about a task force? Who's overseeing it, funding it? I really don't like this." She pressed her hand to her own chest.

Gail made another face and looked down at her coffee. "You know what, Billy Jo? Mark's right about one thing: You should put your feet up and take it easy this morning." She walked over to the coffeepot and refilled her mug. "I think I'm going to grab a quick shower, too."

Then Gail walked away and down the stairs, and Billy Jo realized that for all the questions she had, Gail likely had more. But she would tread only so far down that road back to the horror that had her living with them.

Billy Jo listened to the water running, her husband still in the shower. Mark was holding back something. Whatever it was, she'd do her own digging and find out who had shown up on her doorstep and what kind of team, exactly, they wanted her husband to join.

ABOUT THE AUTHOR

Lorhainne Eckhart, a New York Times & USA Today bestselling author, crafts stories of undeniable intimacy and family drama, earning her the title of "Queen of the family saga." Her works delve deep into the complexities of family dynamics, mingling suspense and angst with a touch of romance to engage readers on multiple levels. Renowned for her 'Raw Relatable Real Romance,' Lorhainne's narratives reflect strong moral themes and the importance of family.

With over 145 titles across multiple series now available in Italian, Spanish, French, and German, Lorhainne continues to captivate a global audience. Her literary contributions have garnered multiple Readers' Favorite Awards for Suspense and Romance. Beyond her writing, she is a mother of three, an advocate for autism awareness, and a believer in pursuing dreams.

Stay updated on her latest releases and promotional offers by following Lorhainne on Bookbub and subscribing to her mailing list at LorhainneEckhart.com, where you can also find her Monday Blog on all things books and life.

"Lorhainne Eckhart has this uncanny way of just hitting the spot every time with her books."

(CAROLINE L., REVIEWER)

Lorhainne loves to hear from her readers! You can connect with me at:
www.LorhainneEckhart.com
lorhainneeckhart.le@gmail.com

facebook.com/AuthorLorhainneEckhart
x.com/LEckhart
instagram.com/lorhainneeckhart
bookbub.com/profile/lorhainne-eckhart
pinterest.com/lorhainneeckhart

SERIES AVAILABLE

Billy Jo McCabe Mystery: The social worker and the cop, an unlikely couple drawn together on a small, secluded Pacific Northwest island where nothing is as it seems

The Watchers: Six unlikely friends, with a diverse set of skills, are brought together to face off against a common enemy in the mind-bending new series The Watchers.

The Friessen Legacy: Embrace heartwarming Friessen family love across three series, *The Outsider, The Friessens: A New Beginning and The Friessens*

The McCabe Brothers: Join the five McCabe siblings on their journeys to the dark and dangerous side of love.

The O'Connells: Journey into Love and Danger with the unconventional O'Connells of Montana

The Parker Sisters: Small-Town Love and sisterly bonds: Join the Parker Sisters of Wyoming on their heartfelt journey to finding Love

The Street Fighter: Welcome to the gripping world of the Streetfighter mystery series where justice is a battle fought on the mean streets and in the corridors of power

The Wilde Brothers: Enter the world of the Wilde Brothers a captivating Idaho family saga of romance rugged charm and strong bonds.

Walk the Right Road: Featuring a faked death, a dangerous choice and more, this stunning series of love and suspense will take you on an irresistible journey

The Saved Series: Love, danger and survival: Join Abby and Eric for a riveting journey of heart-pounding romance and suspense

Kate & Walker: Dive into a suspenseful romance series with Kate & Walker.

Married in Montana: Discover Heartfelt Romance and Second Chances in the Married in Montana Series

ALSO BY LORHAINNE ECKHART

The Outsider Series
The Forgotten Child
A Baby and a Wedding *(An Outsider Series Short)*
Fallen Hero
The Awakening
Secrets
Runaway
Overdue *(An Outsider Series Short)*
The Unexpected Storm
The Wedding

The Friessens: A New Beginning
The Deadline
The Price to Love
A Different Kind of Love
A Vow of Love, A Friessen Family Christmas

The Friessens
The Reunion
The Bloodline
The Promise
The Business Plan
The Decision
First Love
Family First
Leave the Light On
In the Moment
In the Family

In the Silence
In the Charm
Unexpected Consequences
It Was Always You
The First Time I Saw You
Welcome to My Arms
Welcome to Boston
I'll Always Love You
Ground Rules
A Reason to Breathe
You Are My Everything
Anything For You
The Homecoming
Stay Away From My Daughter
The Bad Boy
A Place of Our Own
The Visitor
All About Devon
Long Past Dawn
How to Heal a Heart
Keep Me In Your Heart

The O'Connells
The Neighbor
The Third Call
The Secret Husband
The Quiet Day
The Commitment
The Missing Father
The Hometown Hero
Justice
The Family Secret
The Fallen O'Connell

The Return of the O'Connells
And The She Was Gone
The Stalker
The O'Connell Family Christmas
The Girl Next Door
Broken Promises
The Gatekeeper
The Hunted

The McCabe Brothers
Don't Stop Me (Vic)
Don't Catch Me (Chase)
Don't Run From Me (Aaron)
Don't Hide From Me (Luc)
Don't Leave Me (Claudia)
Out of Time

A Billy Jo McCabe Mystery
Nothing As it Seems
Hiding in Plain Sight
The Cold Case
The Trap
Above the Law
The Stranger at the Door
The Children
The Last Stand
The Charity
The Sacrifice

The Watchers
Shadow Game

The Wilde Brothers

The One (Joe and Margaret)
The Honeymoon, A Wilde Brothers Short
Friendly Fire (Logan and Julia)
Not Quite Married, A Wilde Brothers Short
A Matter of Trust (Ben and Carrie)
The Reckoning, A Wilde Brothers Christmas
Traded (Jake)
Unforgiven (Samuel)
The Holiday Bride

Married in Montana
His Promise
Love's Promise
A Promise of Forever

The Parker Sisters
Thrill of the Chase
The Dating Game
Play Hard to Get
What We Can't Have
Go Your Own Way
A June Wedding

Kate & Walker
One Night
Edge of Night
Last Night

Walk the Right Road Series
The Choice
Lost and Found
Merkaba
Bounty

Blown Away: The Final Chapter
He Came Back

The Saved Series
Saved
Vanished
Captured

Single Titles
Loving Christine

www.ingramcontent.com/pod-product-compliance
Lightning Source LLC
Chambersburg PA
CBHW032306310726
48973CB00008B/2541